De

AK Cooper-Elliot

Table of Contents

DEDICATION

I dedicate this book to my late father. He insp_red me to work hard and always do my best. Thanks, Dad.

ACKNOWLEDGMENTS

I want to express my special thanks to my son Sam who lives in New Zealand, for his creative graphic designs. A huge hug for my daughter Georgina.

Thank you to my mum and husband, who have given me so much support and love over the last year whilst writing this book.

And as always, keeping my feet warm under the desk, my dog Willow.

ABOUT THE AUTHOR

AK Cooper-Elliot was born in Germany and raised in Yorkshire. After graduating from university in the early nineties, Cooper-Elliot pursued a high-flying career in Accountancy & Procurement. Retiring early from her executive role, she now creates exciting romantic and crime novels in her home office.

DECESSUS

The cessation of life

An end to an organism's existence

A star fades away and explodes like a supernova.

PROLOGUE

Templeton House - Zurich - Switzerland

16th January 2000

Two men and two women stood before two brass caskets. Allison, dressed in black, wearing a woollen swing dress, stared in silence at the late couple. Her eyes began to drip, but this time no stylist came to apply new make-up.

At her side, outfitted with a matching crossover, Annie Brown-Templeton-Miller concealed her tears beneath a black veil. Henry and Richard Templeton-Miller displayed wrinkled morning suits, still unbuttoned.

Eleanor had passed away in her sleep at the age of seventy-nine, on 12th January 2000. Theo-James died in his sleep two days later at the age of eighty-four, heartbroken. The Templeton-Miller children crumbled by the loss of both parents within days of one another.

The film industry paid its respects by honouring Theo-James and Eleanor's movies on TV. The whole world lit candles in vigils of mourning for the two lovers.

Not one person was allowed into the sitting room. Years of memories buried there, and the children would only allow visitors on the day of the funeral. Grandchildren, friends, and the Templeton-Miller spouses were even ruled out.

Allison and her siblings became duplicates of one another, and their spouses were amazed how they had changed into authoritarians. Far from the world, the four siblings became closer together.

Romano worried for his wife Allison and stayed close to his in-laws, Rene, Ami, and Ricky. Their children, who were now adults or nearly adults, remained together.

Nineteen-year-old Nathaniel Templeton-Mancini had told his cousins that their parents were turning into zombies. This accusation upset Ella-Louisa, now fourteen, and Romano severely punished his son by confiscating his mobile phone.

Masses of media camped outside Templeton House. Ladders erected against the gigantic rustic wall. Ultra-large cameras, huge macro lenses, broadcasting cameras, and handheld microphones surrounded the scene. Groups of winter-clad men and women chatted, smoked, and talked on their mobile phones while stamping their feet on the icy snow.

Sebastian Dupont, now fifty-nine, composed himself as he approached the cast-iron gates. Two individuals …accompanied him.

Thirty-nine-year-old Bentley St Lavigne had become Allison's new-fangled manager. Working under the influence of Sebastian Dupont, the music and film executive showed his professionalism towards the superstar. Allison indicated her apathetic mood concerning the alteration of her management team.

Hardy Thompson-Jones, Mr St Lavigne's personal assistant, followed his master. Both gents dressed in designer suits from the house of Sylvester-Montgomery. Sporting short haircuts and spectacles, they duplicated Sebastian.

Security opened the whining cast-iron gates, and the three classy gentlemen offered themselves up to the ravenous press.

"Good morning. I wish to update you regarding the Templeton-Millers. A private funeral will be held at St Paul's Chapel tomorrow at 11:00 a.m. The family have restricted attendance to close friends and associates. I will say on this occasion that certain clientele of the film world will not be in attendance. Please respect the family's privacy during this distressing time. Thank you for your discretion." Sebastian folded the perfumed pink notepaper with his leather-gloved hands and returned it to his pocket.

Camera flashes continued to ignite the area while various reporters aimed their microphones toward Sebastian, shouting irrelevant questions. Turning his back on the media, he casually strolled with his cane towards Templeton House. Tearing up the note paper, he snarled, "I'm sure she does this purposely."

Bentley responded, "Allison is a fool. Writing on perfumed paper is not at all professional."

Hardy paced up to the glamourous twosome. "Annie wrote the note using Eleanor's bureau."

"She's still a fool," Bentley muttered, pacing alongside Sebastian.

Sebastian gazed forward, facing the iconic house. "Bentley, my darling, you have your work cut out with Alice. I'm not sure how she is going to react after the funeral. She changed dramatically when her friend Fay passed away My time has passed, too. I would fully retire, but the limelight is good for my skin."

"Sebastian, my dear friend, organising Allison's schedule over the past two years has given me agita. Extending the Mancini studio was a step forward, I thought, but Mani-Music Record Label was just the start of our catastrophe. We have five music technicians including Josh Williams, and Marc Garcia. But she still refuses to cut the album *I Will Never Look Back*." Bentley said.

"Don't look back, Bentley," Sebastian chuckled.

"She has now promised to cut the album next month with Josh and Marc," Hardy added.

"Alice's promises are as reliable as her sleep schedule. Darling, do you think she is going to cut the album next month? You have two great record producers. It's a shame Marc veered into car racing: he could have joined the team much earlier to help the dynamic duo." Sebastian continued crunching ice beneath his cane.

"Allison is still the top artist in the western world." Bentley cut in with his pure aristocratic English accent.

Entering the foyer and removing his coat, Sebastian faced Bentley and Hardy. "She's eccentric, Lavigne. All artists are. Alice isn't just a client: she's my friend and will continue to be, until death."

****

St Paul's Chapel - Zurich - Switzerland

17th January 2000

Two bronze caskets, timeless and elegant, were supported by several pallbearers. The family followed behind, walking upon the embankments of snow. The four siblings disregarded everything around them and trailed behind their parents.

Romano walked with his children, supporting a tearful Ella-Louisa. Nathaniel convinced his younger brother, Benedict, that their mother had been snatched by aliens.

The family remained closely behind Romano. Sebastian, Oliver, Bentley, and Hardy persisted even farther back. The friends of Eleanor and Theo-James placed themselves at the far rear of the procession. Craig Welling and the rest of Templeton security walked at either side of the family, obscuring any media intrusion.

Inside the small, dimly lit chapel, the caskets were placed next to one another in the soleas. Four siblings took their places in the first pew while their spouses and children sat behind. Henry Templeton-Miller instructed Father Egger to conduct the briefest service available.

Fifteen minutes later, the service had concluded. Silence swallowed the sniffling and muted sobs. The four siblings removed themselves from their positions in the first pew and lit a candle each. The pallbearers carried the caskets along the small aisle towards the entrance doors.

The Templeton-Millers had procured a family tomb. The grey stone monument was located privately at the rear of the chapel, surrounded by spruces.

Tomb engravings consisted of airborne angels hovering with their harps towards heaven. Two Victorian lanterns flickered at either side of the entrance, while a three-seater stone bench sat abandoned, suffocating in snow.

The caskets disappeared down the stone steps into the depths of the tomb. Only the four siblings followed, each carrying one solitary white rose. Standing inside the chamber, they placed two roses upon each casket. The siblings recited The Lord's Prayer and returned up the stone steps. Allison stopped and asked the cemetery officials for five minutes alone.

Allison remained with her parents by herself. Eleanor and Theo- James laid side by side on a stone outcropping designed by Theo-James himself.

Allison stopped and glanced at the official, standing observing by the entrance steps. She placed a delicate kiss on each casket. A single tear rolled down her apricot cheek.

"I know you are proud of me, but I cannot continue with my career. It makes me so miserable, and I'm only living because of my husband and children. Help me to grow strong without music, without films."

A sudden breeze surged towards her petite frame. Allison released a deep sigh and looked up at the ceiling. "I can feel you both. Thank you for understanding…I love you."

Placing her veil over her face again, she followed the official up the steps. Reaching daylight, she continued to walk towards her beautiful husband and children.

Squeezed between her family, she sniffled. "You are my joy, my world, my life."

Romano removed her veil. Witnessing her glowing, watering, red eyes, he kissed the top of her forehead. "You are mine, always."

****

CHAPTER 1

Mancini Mansion - New Jersey

16th March 2000 - 10.30 a.m.

The crystal chandeliers illuminated oil paintings of the Mancini family hanging on gold and silver walls. Abandoned in the centre of the room stood a handcrafted walnut dining table.

Burrows & Burrows Lawyers Andrew Mason-Edwards and Patrick Jones-Gustav walked into the dining room and selected one of the thirty brass-studded high back chairs. Douglas Black and Donald Gooding, Argentum Banking Group, followed the two lawyers and placed themselves opposite.

Sebastian Dupont and Bentley St Lavigne conversed in the marbled foyer, while Oliver Dupont arranged coffee, tea, and iced water with Simons and his staff. Hardy Thompson-Jones transported documents into the dining room, nodding at the reputable businessmen arranging paperwork. Hardy coordinated stationery and files at the end of the lengthy polished table.

"Good morning, gentlemen," a female voice vibrated across the vast room.

Andrew Mason-Edwards removed himself from his chair and offered her the seat. "Morning, Mrs Mancini."

Allison strolled towards the end of the table, wearing a black Sylvester-Montgomery blazer dress. Her dark hair swept back into an up-do. Intense red lipstick gave colour to her pale complexion,

Sebastian and Oliver Dupont walked behind Allison as Simons and his team followed with trays of assorted beverages. Taking their places, Sebastian displayed the elegancy of his usual pink cravat. Oliver sported a black tweed suit and grey silk tie from the same designers.

"Shall we begin?" Allison announced from the end of the table while opening a leather-bound file that Hardy had handed her.

Douglas Black coughed and commenced with the discussion. "Mrs Mancini..."

"Please, call me Alice," she interrupted him. "With the death of Templeton, I am no longer Allison Templeton-Miller. Just Alice!"

Douglas Black flushed with embarrassment.

"Alice, the legacy involving your parent's wealth has valuated into a situation..."

"Speak English!" Allison interrupted Douglas.

Andrew Mason-Edwards cut in, "Miss Alice, you are now the richest woman in the world."

"Richest woman? So, there are still men ahead of me?" Allison tapped her manicured red fingernails against the wooden table. “I don’t need Mama and Papa’s inheritance. Keep it.”

“Eleanor’s dying wish was to bequeath her estate to you. Our team have some suggestions about how to spend it.” Donald Gooding replied. “This is not investment advice, but…”

The double walnut doors opened, and Bentley St Lavigne paced in. “Sorry for my retardation.”

Allison glared at him while he placed himself next to the superstar. Sebastian grinned with pleasure. Both he and Oliver were loving the show. Pouring himself an Earl Grey tea, Sebastian continued to observe the meeting with interest.

“The only retardation here is that this meeting hasn’t concluded.” Allison smiled.

“We don’t understand…” Douglas intervened.

“Hardy, please permit the files to each guest, please,” Allison announced.

The four suited businessmen opened each file as it was placed before them. Studying the documentation inside the laminated folders, the glamourous dining room was thrown into an unnatural silence.

Sebastian and Oliver Dupont opened their copies and suddenly glanced at the three figures sitting at the top of the table.

"My career in show business is over!" Allison said, removing herself from her chair. Walking around the dining room with her hands behind her back, she continued to explain her actions. "I did some shopping. Or as you men call it, an acquisition. I am now the owner of Sphere Pictures."

Sebastian spat out his tea all over his folder. Searching for his handkerchief, Oliver began to dab the remnants of Earl Grey from Sebastian's file.

Allison continued, "Sphere will be operated by twelve directors, who all answer to me, majority shareholder! The presidentess." Allison walked towards the double casement doors, concealed behind opaque gardenia velvet drapes, and curtsied. "The company, or, more accurately, my company, will be called Millers-Sphere Films." Turning around again, she continued, "My grandpapa owned Miller-Lions Corporation. Unfortunately, my papa rented it to Sphere Pictures. My task is done, the film company is back within the family."

"How did you wire the money?" Douglas Black asked.

"Money? I bought it on credit," Allison replied, brandishing her purse.

Oliver spluttered water out of his mouth, and Sebastian assisted with the clean-up operation.

"The board said I should consult a lawyer first, but that's no way to talk to the presidentess! All contracts and submissions went through Battie & Thomas." Allison continued, "If you observe the transaction in January, there was a small transfer of two billion dollars."

Sebastian was on the verge of having a cardiac arrest when Donald cut in, "Two billion dollars?"

"Oh, I almost forgot. Green Records! I purchased that too…"

Andrew Mason-Edwards nearly fainted. Patrick Jones-Gustav dabbed water on his face to wake him up.

"May 1980, Mani-Music was born, thanks to Mr Dupont and Josh Williams. My five-year contract had ended with Green. Was always my least-favourite colour anyway. Unfortunately for Josh and myself, Green Records extended the contract by ten months due to our graduation at Kellie… Green Records is sadly no more. Oops, the company is now called Mani-Music Productions." Allison smiled and walked toward her shocked attorneys.

"Michael Lyon-Simmons," Sebastian said.

"Yes, not only is he an excellent defence lawyer, but he also always does what I say," Allison smirked.

Oliver raised an eyebrow.

"What about Bentley and Hardy?" Sebastian replied, looking at the two refined men at the top of the table.

“They work for me…Bentley and Hardy are my PAs!”

“And us?” Sebastian said, pointing at Oliver and himself.

“Open page ten.” Allison said. “Enjoy your retirement.”

Sebastian doubled glanced at the paperwork, “You have purchased Aquifolium Mansion in New Jersey?”

“Yes, the cost-per-syllable was a steal. Donald, please refer to the transaction: fifty million dollars, your retirement package from me! Also, today I will be depositing another fifty million into your bank account, but only if someone refills my teacup.”

Sebastian became pale and insisted on a glass of water.

“Any designer and furniture paid by me…. Oops, I keep forgetting, you have a Ferrari 599 GTB ordered, one each, black!” Allison smiled. “It goes with everything. I will continue. Josh Williams is one of the directors with Marc Garcia. Both will administer control of the production, operating in New Jersey and in LA. Donald, Douglas, Andrew, Patrick, I will still require your services. Firstly…”

“We just say ‘first’ around here. What about Battie?” Douglas cut in.

“Battie & Thomas will be assisting Burrows & Burrows with my next contracts.”

“Contracts!”

“Yes, I am founding an academy for young adults to learn about the industry and gain experience working in apprenticeships. The film and record industries are struggling."

"They're not the only ones who are struggling!" Andrew chipped in, loosening his tie.

"Now that I own Millers-Sphere and Mani-Music Productions, we can link the academies all over the states."

"Oh, you mean the schools!" Oliver announced.

"My other investment, see page fifteen. Education in the Third World." Allison said.

"You mean more schools?" Andrew, Douglas, Donald, and Patrick blurted.

"Excuse me, I prefer to continue without interruptions." Allison said, retaking her seat. "Likewise, I would like to invest in the Kellie School of Performing Arts."

"H…How much?" Sebastian stuttered.

"I want to run a programme for all the students from a poor background. The disadvantaged ones, too."

"Grants?" Sebastian replied.

"No, I'm not giving grants: I'm granting wishes," Allison announced.

"Good God," Andrew said. "She's lost it."

Sebastian, Oliver, Hardy, Bentley, Burrows & Burrows, and Argentum Banking Group stood up and checked their pulses to see if they had died and gone to Hell.

“Meeting adjourned!” she bowed. “Now who wants champagne?”

The dining room doors opened, and Romano returned with a tray of champagne glasses, followed by Simons with three emerald bottles.

“Gentlemen, celebrations are in order!” Romano winked at Allison. Romano, nearly fifty, opened a bottle of champagne as old as he was and poured it into ten flutes.

The greying but still handsome children’s author raised his glass towards his wife. “To Allison Templeton-Mancini, the presidentess!”

Allison raised her glass: “To Fay!”

****

Mancini Mansion - 1.30 p.m.

“Alice, my darling, that was a delightful surprise!” Sebastian said, buttering his soup roll using a vintage sterling silver knife.

“Sebastian, nearly sixty? You’re retiring in your prime!” Allison smiled, pointing her finger towards her friends. “Purchasing a house next door, I can keep an eye on the two of you.”

Romano poured sparkling champagne into four glass flutes while the Mancini staff continued to serve pumpkin soup.

“You have always amazed me, Alice. I still want the inside scoop regarding your investments,” Oliver announced.

“Inside trading, Oliver? Naughty boy. When I fly out to visit my schools, you are coming with me.”

“Maybe I’ll call in sick!” he replied, sipping his cool champagne.

“My husband will tag along for the break,” Sebastian said.

Romano, already eating his soup, added, “I thought you guys would retire together!”

“No, there’s still much to achieve. I’m only going to retire when Alice is six feet under,” Oliver laughed.

“Under what?” Allison scoffed.

“Eleanor was the only thing keeping my wife in line,” Romano chuckled.

“*Conception Magazine* profits billions of dollars from Alice and will continue to even after her decease, should that ever occur.” Oliver grinned. “By the way, this soup is delicious!”

Allison sighed, listening to the birds sing. “Sebastian is travelling to London next month. He is auditioning for the West End!”

Sebastian Dupont dropped his spoon. “Who’s his manager?” he asked.

"Bentley!" Allison announced with a grin. "Romano and I are travelling with him on the Mancini Jet, apartment hunting!"

"You should have said so. I sold my apartment in Camden a few years ago." Sebastian said.

"The Atrium Apartments were beautiful, but I want him to live near the theatre." Romano dabbed his mouth with a napkin.

"Understandable. We are keeping Alexander House. Oliver will reside there whilst working in New York. I will endeavour to assist with the design of Aquifolium Mansion." Sebastian smiled.

Allison counted the syllables on her fingers.

"How are the rest of the children?" Oliver asked.

"Benedict is performing at an excellent rate with his tennis. Ella-Louisa is modelling for Sylvester-Montgomery." Allison cleared her throat; the loss of Phillippe upset her immensely. Fabian-Astor-Sylvester and Miles Montgomery became his replacement and instantly became best friends with Allison.

Allison continued, "Nathaniel graduated with his brothers to pursue acting. Rupert is going to be an assistant director to Stephen-Paul Golding."

Oliver and Sebastian looked in shock. "Stephen is a director?" Sebastian said.

"And one of my shareholders…" Allison added.

"Millers-Sphere!" replied Oliver.

"Yes, Nathaniel is guaranteed a part in their next movie, with Rupert as the assistant director. The triplets will be twenty in November."

"When do they officially graduate?" Sebastian asked.

"May!" Romano stepped in. "Their grades have exceeded expectations."

Sebastian looked at Oliver again. "Where have I been over the past few years? Time has flown by so quickly…I feel old."

Romano laughed. "I'm greyer than you…"

Destroying his bread roll, Oliver replied, "We have a great hairdresser."

CHAPTER 2

Montrose Gatehouse II - Mayfair - London

16th March 2004 - 8.00 a.m.

Sebastian Templeton-Mancini stretched out naked on top of his king-sized bed, cuddling a red-haired woman. Stroking her soft skin, he kissed her on the chest before removing himself from his relaxed position. Stepping into the bathroom, he reached inside the shower and turned on the faucets.

The door opened behind him. A pair of cool, delicate hands wrapped around the knob and turned up the heat. Steam blurred the mirror, still reflecting the silhouette of a soft female body pressing up against him. They kissed.

"I'm supposed to be filming in a couple of hours..." Sarah groaned, dropping her head onto Sebastian's toned shoulder.

"Not with me, I hope." Sebastian said, shampooing his hair. "Performance anxiety."

"I meant for television, silly!"

Sarah-Jane washed Sebastian's back with a loofah and continued placing lavender soap on his olive skin. "Dad is out of the acting business, and he seems to be a lot better."

"Yep! Mom signed him up yesterday. Mani-Music Productions," Sebastian moaned in pleasure while the soap dripped from his body.

"A director! Dad has shares!"

"Moms had it all worked out!" Sebastian declared. "Your turn!"

Sarah-Jane turned around, and Sebastian placed the lavender soap between her breasts.

"Sebastian! No more...I will be late!"

A knock at the bedroom door startled Sarah-Jane. "Miss Belling-Davis, your car is waiting."

"In a minute!" Sarah yelled, and she opened the shower door, releasing the steam into the white-tiled bathroom.

Sebastian laughed, following her out into the bedroom. Tying a towel around his waist, he walked towards the bedroom door. Sarah-Jane's security officer Max faked a smile as he ran a metal detector over Sebastian's groin.

"Very funny, Max." Sebastian's raven hair dripped water onto the polished oak flooring.

"Can't be too safe, Sebastian," Max winked.

Max B-Turner was Sarah-Jane's English bodyguard, aged thirty-five. Always immaculately dressed in dark suits and very handsome with platinum blonde hair and blue eyes. Max's height was identical to Sebastian.

Walking into the kitchen, Max turned on the chrome kettle switch and opened the cupboard to retrieve a jar of instant coffee.

“Make that two,” Melvin Davis-Grey said, taking his seat at the black gloss island.

“I thought you Americans didn’t like instant!” Max replied.

“We don’t like London, either, but we’re still here!” Melvin fist-bumped Max.

Craig Welling recruited American Melvin Davis-Grey, twenty-nine, as personal bodyguard to Sebastian. Both men resided at Montrose Gatehouse II and were single. Melvin tall like Max trained regularly in the gym.

“The driver is peeved waiting for Sarah,” Max said, handing over a black coffee to Melvin.

“Women!” he laughed.

“Have you seen the new neighbour? She’s a knockout,” Max grinned. “Tall, auburn hair, not natural, big breasts.”

“Older women are very attractive!”

“I would say she is around mid-fifties,” Max grinned. “She’s got a son, looks about eighteen, but I haven’t seen a guy with her.”

“Not yet,” Melvin winked, adding milk to his steaming coffee.

Sebastian stepped into the kitchen wearing his usual skinny jeans and tailored black shirt. “Tea on the go?”

“Yeah, we offer Earl Grey and…” Max checked the cupboard. “Earl Grey.”

"You know, you are the double of your dad!" Melvin said.

"No, Nat is Dad's double, even combs his fingers through his hair like him," Sebastian replied.

"I remember you two when you were small." Melvin grinned. "Sylvester clothing!"

"Oh, they were fun times. Rup used to beat us up before our shoot!" Sebastian howled.

"He's the small one!" Max replied.

"Sure is," Sebastian grinned.

"Benedict is doing well, US junior champion..." Melvin smiled, sipping another mouthful of instant.

"Tennis?" Max said.

"Yep, he's massive," Sebastian whistled.

"Your mum has quit music. I have all her albums. Templeton too," Max said, handing Sebastian his tea.

"She quit after her friend died, never got over it. Walked right off the set!"

"I'm ready, Max," shouted Sarah-Jane from the staircase.

"Certainly!" Max called back, removing his huge body from his Cuban chair.

Sebastian hurried into the chequered foyer. Helping Sarah-Jane with her jacket, he leaned in and kissed her. Max waited by the lounge door.

"Ready, Miss Belling-Davis?" he nodded.

Sebastian sighed while his love disappeared into a black Mercedes C-Class.

****

Montrose Gatehouse II - Mayfair - London

16th March 2004 - 1.30 p.m.

Sebastian stretched out along his luxury king-sized bed, staring at his silver laptop. An aristocratic English accent rang through the speakers:

"The show is going on Broadway in October. Your options are to stay put or carry on with the show in New York," said the executive.

"London is my home. Sarah-Jane's work is here. I cannot be apart from her, Bentley."

"My darling Sebastian, you do sound like your father!"

"And you sound like Sebastian Dupont!" Sebastian growled.

Bentley coughed while adjusting his round metal spectacles. "My boy, I do have another option. Do Broadway for six months and stay at the Palmer Building. Sarah-Jane can use the Mancini Jet."

Sebastian cut in, "Mom, are you there?"

Allison appeared on the screen displaying her charm and charisma. "Sebastian, the show is only running for a year on Broadway. There is another show soon in London."

"Mom, what have you done?" Sebastian said, annoyed.

"Charles Medley-Garrett requires a male lead for *Beyond Anything*. It's going to be huge!"

"And I take it you have agreed for me to audition for the part," Sebastian scoffed.

"Well, he did approach Bentley with an understanding that you may remain in your current show," Allison smiled.

"Think about it, Sebastian, you will remain in London with Sarah-Jane," Bentley said.

"Mom! I will visit, I promise. I just always thought that the Palmer Building was Nat's!"

"Why do you say that?" Allison replied, staring through her glasses.

"Rup and I call it his love shack!" Sebastian laughed.

"I don't like the sound of that." Allison scoffed. "He is always in LA; we have given him Porta Del Castello. Rupert lives next door, Santiago Del Porto. Much smaller place, five bedrooms, but it agrees with Rupert."

Sebastian laughed again. "Rup and Nat are always together." Glancing out of the sash windows, he noticed rain spotting against the glass. "I do miss the American sunshine!"

"Can we continue with a new contract, or do we keep the old one and move you to New York?" Bentley interrupted his thoughts.

"I am going to discuss this with Sarah-Jane," Sebastian said, playing with the floral duvet cover. "Tonight, after my performance."

"Okay. I shall video call tomorrow," Bentley announced.

Allison blew him a kiss through the computer screen and waved goodbye.

Sebastian closed his laptop and grunted. "How old I'm I? Nearly twenty-four and they act like I'm four! I'm getting bloody married!"

Storming off downstairs, he ordered a car to take him to the local registry office. A black Mercedes C Class waited outside the Edwardian structure of Montrose Gatehouse II. Sebastian stepped outside wearing dark sunglasses and a long grey raincoat. It was time to organise his life without any interference.

****

The City of London Registry Office.

13th April 2004 - 11.00 a.m.

Sarah-Jane Belling-Davis dressed to perfection in a knee-length white lace dress and matching jacket. Gripping her coordinating clutch bag and white posy, she climbed into the back of the Mercedes.

Following his future wife into the prestigious car, Sebastian sported a Sylvester-Montgomery three-piece in navy blue. Melvin and Max were the couple's associated witnesses. Dressed in their usual dark designer suits, the two bodyguards looked the part.

Sebastian had agreed to continue with the show on Broadway for six months and return to London and sign a new contract with Charles Medley-Garrett. Sarah-Jane agreed she would take six months off work and remain at the Palmer Building with her future husband.

When Sebastian proposed in his dressing room after his show in March. Sarah-Jane cried with acceptance, and the pair excitingly enjoyed an afternoon in London, wedding shopping.

Two diamond wedding rings and an oval ruby ring were ordered. It was important to colour match the engagement ring to Sarah-Jane's hair. Sebastian loved her hair colour and pale skin.

Ascending the stone steps to the Victorian building, Sebastian gripped Sarah-Jane's hand. Pacing through the entrance, trying to avoid any publicity, Sebastian tugged her gently towards a sign that said *Marriages: Second Floor*.

"You, okay?" he smiled at his bride.

"Yes, let's do this!" she nodded.

Entering the aristocratic room, the registrar guided the couple and their witnesses to stand before a solid oak table. Explaining the procedure, the lady registrar placed Sebastian's hands upon Sarah-Jane's. Repeating their vows to one another, the couple were married within fifteen minutes.

Sarah-Jane kissed her new husband delicately before she sat down to sign the register. Two bouquets of fresh cream roses were placed in glass vases on the table next to the couple signing the register. Max and Melvin took snapshots of the new Mr and Mrs Templeton-Mancini.

"Mrs Templeton-Mancini, home!" Sebastian laughed.

"Mrs Belling-Davis-Templeton-Mancini!" she smiled.

Sebastian glared at her. "You're kidding! It's far too long!"

Sarah-Jane laughed, gripping harder onto Sebastian's hand. "Only joking!"

Another pre-marital couple and their family waited outside the amalgamation room.

"Oh my God," whispered the bride wearing a full-length wedding gown. "It's Sebastian Templeton-Mancini!"

Max and Melvin were straight on it. "With us, now!"

The new Mr and Mrs Templeton-Mancini escaped along a panelled oak corridor and down another set of red-carpeted stairs. The two bodyguards checked for clearance and noticed paparazzi lingering in the foyer.

"Damn, press!" Max grunted.

Melvin grabbed an official and explained the situation of the power couple. She obliged to help, with a signed autograph from Sebastian and Sarah-Jane. Opening a fire door at the rear of the building, Max radioed for the Mercedes to meet them in the alleyway.

The Mercedes appeared from out of nowhere, and the newlyweds, plus both bodyguards, jumped into the car before speeding off. Turning the corner, Sarah-Jane gasped! There were paparazzi everywhere, and the couple ducked their heads below the blacked-out windows.

Living at Montrose: the security was excellent. Both ends of the road were fenced off by electronic security gates, and only a swipe card would allow you through the entrance onto the street. Onlookers were massing in the middle of the road.

"Oh no!" Sarah-Jane moaned, hugging Sebastian as the vehicle swerved to avoid the crowd.

"Press, TV, Mom's fans, just great!" he glared through the rear glass.

Max and Melvin jumped out of the vehicle and ran towards the gate, creating a barrier against the press.

"I don't know how you live with this," Sarah-Jane muttered.

"You're not divorcing me already?"

"Would I be the first?"

The car delivered the newlyweds to their home, and the couple disappeared inside their luxury London house.

Sebastian's house employed no staff but a pair of bodyguards. A professional cleaning company did come to the house and operate its cleaning service, including the laundry.

While the newlyweds removed their jackets in the foyer, the answering machine flashed. Sebastian noticed the glimmering red light and pressed play. A sharp beep echoed while the agitated voice of Romano Mancini urgently requested Sebastian to call him back.

"I'm going in his bad books!" Sebastian scoffed, picking up the receiver to dial his father.

Sebastian waited for his call to be connected.

"Dad, what time is it over there?" Sebastian chuckled, trying to break the ice.

"I have just watched the seven o'clock news, and you..."

"Got married. Sarah-Jane is now Mrs Templeton-Mancini." Sebastian blew a kiss towards his wife.

"Congratulations, son! You know this will upset your mom. She would have wanted you to have a huge wedding. Belinda, will be a pain in the butt."

"Dad, you have always known that Sarah-Jane and I have been childhood sweethearts."

"I know. I thought you would have done it sooner!" Romano replied. "I would have married your mom sooner, but it had to be the wedding of the year!"

"Are you going to break it to her?" Sebastian said,

"If the TV doesn't first," Romano said, ringing off.

Sarah-Jane walked into the foyer, wearing an apron over her wedding dress. "I'm cooking brunch, pancakes!"

****

Mancini Manson - New Jersey

13th April 2004 - 9.00 a.m.

Allison strolled down the staircase, wearing fluffy pink slippers and a coordinating dressing gown. Her dark locks bounced maliciously against her shoulders.

Simons addressed his mistress, "Breakfast is served on the terrace."

"Thank you, Simons," said Allison. "Another beautiful day."

Strolling towards the fully bloomed terrace, she noticed Romano fiddling with a white linen napkin.

"Morning!"

Romano looked up. "Morning, baby!"

"So, spill the beans!" Allison giggled, taking a seat across from her handsome husband.

Romano hesitantly smiled and spoke. "Sebastian..."

"Is married!" Allison announced, placing her napkin on her lap.

"How do you know?" Romano blurted in full surprise.

"Belinda told me two weeks ago!"

"Two weeks?" Romano said, two pitches higher than his usual tone.

"Sarah-Jane let it slip."

"Belinda?"

"Overjoyed! We are all planning a wedding reception when they arrive in October," Allison said, accepting her scrambled eggs on toast.

"Where?"

Allison laughed. "Here, silly! Sarah-Jane is having a gown designed by Sylvester-Montgomery. She doesn't know it yet," Allison beamed. "Belinda's idea."

Romano shook his head. "You and Belinda still amaze me even after all these years."

"Best friends for life." Allison crunched on her toast and winked at Romano. "Now we're related, too."

CHAPTER 3

Mancini Mansion - New Jersey

9th October 2004 - 6.00 p.m.

Sarah-Jane Templeton-Mancini observed the chaos inside the grand Regency bedroom. Fabian Astor-Sylvester and his team had designed a tailored crepe sheath dress exhibiting a small train and complementary long sleeves.

Placing a diamond ferronnière onto her forehead, Fabian and his staff applauded, while Oliver Dupont and his photographers captured the moment on camera.

Belinda sniffled, sitting on the edge of the classical king-sized bed. Allison sat next to her friend holding a cup and saucer of Earl Grey tea.

“I feel like a medieval princess,” Sarah said.

“You look like one too,” Belinda sniffled into the tissue that Allison had just passed over to her.

“Belinda, your makeup will run!” Allison chuckled.

“I can’t help it!” she said, blowing her nose.

“Alice, Belinda, you’re next,” said Oliver in his burgundy tuxedo.

“I need a stunt double!” Belinda panicked.

“Makeup!” shouted Oliver.

Within seconds two makeup artists from *Conception Magazine* ran into the room and grabbed Belinda.

Allison crumpled with laughter, spilling her tea. Observing the puffs of powder and setting spray, Sarah-Jane just glanced up at the ceiling in despair.

Oliver removed Allison's teacup and pulled her up from the bed. Wearing a silver backless evening gown, Allison Templeton-Mancini looked like a 1940's movie star.

Belinda, wearing a silk-feathered evening gown had her hair curled into ringlets, and diamantes were pinned above the loose waving strands.

"With all these feathers, I look like a chicken!" she huffed, staring at the evening gown in the mirror.

"Darling, this is one of my top designs!" Fabian frowned.

"It looks great..." Allison smiled, taking her place next to the bride.

Sarah-Jane whispered into Allison's ear. "Mom is a pain at times, I'm glad I take after my dad."

Allison burst into laughter, and Sarah-Jane joined her.

"Smile!" Oliver said, snapping the photo.

****

Sebastian, Nathaniel, Rupert, and Benedict chortled over beers in the burgundy sitting room. Sporting black tuxedos, the brothers recounted their memories in the great house.

The four Mancini brothers were nearly identical: raven hair, brown eyes, and olive skin. Height was the key factor that made them different. Rupert was the smallest and

Benedict the tallest, but all remained over six-feet tall apart from Rupert at five-foot-eleven.

A pair of Roman pillars flanked the sitting room. Rose garlands ran down the main staircase, and an archway of assorted fresh flowers covered the main entrances.

Three immense black marquees stood erected on the lawns with various types of roses climbing up the exteriors. The primary marquee arranged thirty round ivory linen tables. The centre pieces flaunted crystal pillars of white roses.

Crystal champagne fountains flowed around a six-tier wedding cake. Cream roses and ivory silk sashes drooped along the ceiling, while five crystal chandeliers twinkled against the evening sunlight seeping through the entrance.

The music marquee's inviting presence ignited the scene with a multicoloured dance floor and rotating disco balls. Next door, the food marquee prepared expensive gourmet food from around the world. Seven chefs and waiting staff prepared themselves for service. Mancini staff escorted the guests onto the terrace, where lanterns scattered the gardens like fireflies.

Ella-Louisa knocked on the door of her grandparents, Maria, and Giuseppe Mancini. Her raven hair curled over her red satin fishtail evening dress.

Maria opened the door and shouted, "Ella!"

Her grandfather pulled her into a hug. She adjusted his dickie bow.

"You look great," she said, shaking the old man's hand.

He smiled, leaned in, and kissed Ella on the side of her cheek. "*Si.*"

Maria laughed in her pink evening gown. "Your grandpapa doesn't like bows!"

"I barely like a suit!" he added in broken English.

Within minutes Ella had tied the perfect bow, and Giuseppe pulled on his blue evening jacket. Holding out his hands, he announced in gratification: "I shall escort my two beautiful women to the ball, one on each arm."

"How romantic, Grandpapa," Ella replied, walking along the floral passageway.

Romano glanced up the grand staircase and noticed his parents and Ella-Louisa. Stopping his conversation with Simons, he whispered, "Mama, Papa?"

"Romano!" his mother cried out when she had reached the bottom step. Grabbing her son by his cheeks, she kissed him. "My son! You look *bellissima!*"

"Mama, Papa, Ella!" he beamed.

"Like the tux, Dad!" Ella smiled.

"White is a classy colour," Romano winked.

"Mom is coming!" Ella said, clapping her hands.

Allison walked down the staircase, escorting a small silver train trickling behind her steps.

"Wow!" Romano gazed at her.

"Husband!" she giggled.

Belinda and Donny Davis strolled down the staircase together.

Sebastian anticipated his bride, standing in the passageway. The door opened, and Fabian invited him into the room. Sarah-Jane stood directly in front of him. He reached out and took her hand with a kiss. "You look beautiful."

Sarah-Jane beamed with happiness. "Not as much as Alice!"

"You like the tux? Red..." he said, grinning at his beautiful bride.

Fabian intervened, "Are you ready?"

Sebastian and Sarah-Jane posed for the *Conception Magazine* cameras and then continued their journey downstairs.

The Mancini brothers and Ella chatted altogether with their parents and grandparents in the flowered foyer. Belinda and Donny installed themselves next to their parents, hoping that the parents wouldn't quarrel.

Melinda Ross-Belling, film actress and Peter Ross-Belling, script writer, divorced in 1979. Melinda had discovered Peter in an uncompromising position between two unnamed actresses.

Belinda thought the gossip would kill her, but her mother hired a brilliant lawyer from Burrows & Burrows. In the divorce settlement, any media or press reports would cost! Peter Ross-Belling had already set fire to his wallet.

Melinda had married film director George Krust. Peter Ross-Belling married former fashion model Mary Gayton, twenty years his junior. Belinda refused to speak to her stepmother.

Sebastian and Sarah-Jane walked down the grand staircase. Camera flashes exploded; *Conception Magazine* shouted out instructions for their grand staircase poses. Selected press continued with their shots for the morning tabloids.

Everyone gasped at the beautiful couple. Romano beamed with pride at his son and his new daughter-in-law. Allison gripped Romano's hand. Maria Mancini wept with happiness. Nathaniel commented that he, too, was going to marry until Ella-Louisa pointed out that first he needed a girlfriend.

When the photographers had finalised their shots, the couple walked out onto the terrace, hand in hand. All the affluent guests were seated at their tables and anticipated the bride and groom. The family followed in pairs behind the happy couple.

Walking into the marquee, the celebrity guests erupted into applause and whistling. The couple took their places at a round table positioned near the elegant wedding cake.

At the next table, Allison and Romano took their places with the clique. The Templeton-Miller siblings settled at table three with Maria and Giuseppe Mancini. Table one entertained the bride and groom with their siblings and cousins.

Peter and Mary were seated with friends from the film industry, which segregated the couple away from Melinda Ross-Belling-Krust. Sebastian's theatre director Charles Medley-Garrett and his daughter Angel were seated at table ten, opposite the bride and groom. Nathaniel Templeton-Mancini had spotted Angel the instant he arrived in the marquee. Deciding to swap seats with his sister Ella, Nathaniel had a clearer view of the beauty that sat opposite.

Chatting with his brothers and cousins, Nathaniel glanced across the table and caught the beauty's eye. Smiling and nodding, he asked a waitress for a pen and paper. Tearing a piece of paper from her order pad, Nathaniel wrote a brief note:

Hi, I am Nat. Can I dance with you later?

Finishing the note with his mobile number. Pointing, he instructed the waitress to give the note to the lady on table ten.

Refusing to take his eye off the waitress, he waited until the beauty read his note. She smiled and mouthed "Yes." A bleep on his mobile sounded. Opening his phone, he read the message:

Hi, my name is Angel Medley-Garrett you now have my mobile number.

Nathaniel's heart raced. Sebastian and Sarah-Jane sliced into their sophisticated white chocolate and diamanté wedding cake. Smiling towards the cameras and Oliver Dupont's team, the beautiful couple embraced with a delicate kiss. Afterwards, imperial waiting staff, dressed in regal-coloured uniforms served food.

Belinda, Lucinda, Adele, Helen, and Allison gossiped over sparkling champagne and seafood risotto.

"You know that Charles Medley-Garrett is gorgeous," Belinda whispered.

"Stop window shopping!" Allison snapped.

"I agree with Belinda," Lucinda jumped in.

"He's Sebastian's boss!"

"He's English!" Belinda announced, sipping her champagne, glancing at the handsome theatre director.

"So?"

"Supposed to be romantic, like King Arthur," Belinda muttered, continuing to stare.

Allison laughed as Lucinda stepped in. "English are said to be good in bed."

"You two are impossible!" Allison sighed.

"What are you three talking about?" Jake grinned.

Belinda shouted, "Sex!"

"Donny, you not servicing your girl?" Sebastian Dupont asked.

Donny dropped his fork. "She's wearing me out!"

Romano consoled his wife's tears. "Belinda, you have set her off again!"

Belinda scoffed, "Not me, my husband!"

Maria and Giuseppe were seated at the next table and noticed the howling of laughter. "I'm so glad we are sat here," she said to Henry Templeton-Miller.

"Maria, I thought table one would be bad with our kids, but we have the biggest kid here," he replied, pointing at his sister, Allison.

Giuseppe Mancini laughed. "*Bambini saranno bambini*."

****

It was time for the first dance, and Allison stepped onto the stage and announced, "Mr and Mrs Templeton-

Mancini." Positioned behind her were five band members: Donny, Marc, Josh, Ricky, and Jack. The whole marquee detonated into screams and cheers. For one night only, Templeton were back.

Sebastian escorted his wife of six months onto the dance floor. Nathaniel scrambled towards Charles Medley-Garrett and asked permission to dance with his daughter.

Allison stepped up to the mic and Josh began to play *Heavenly Body* on the piano. The celebrity audience went silent to the irreplaceable nightingale.

Nathaniel approached Angel and held out his arm with a bow. Angel took his hand, and together they stepped onto the dance floor. Breathing, he pulled her into him.

"I didn't think you'd dance with me," he whispered.

"Why, Nat?" Angel asked, admiring his handsome features.

"I'm not worthy of someone as beautiful as you."

"Because I'm English? Or because I'm not an actress?"

"Because I'm me." Nathaniel gazed down into her sparkling green eyes. "Dinner?"

"It's not going to work! You, a famous movie star, and me, a bank clerk," she stated.

"I'll apply for a job at your bank," he said.

"Pointless, really… me in London, you in LA." Angel paused.

“Stay in touch,” Nathaniel begged.

“Let’s make the most of tonight,” she answered.

Allison ended *Heavenly Body* to wild applause. Bowing to the new Mr and Mrs Templeton-Mancini, she announced the next song: *Breaking Soul.* A rapturous beat sounded, and Ricky and Donny jumped onto their mics with the opening number.

The clique began freaking out with their disco moves on the flashing dance floor, while their kids observed in embarrassment. Romano, Oliver, Jake, Craig, and Sebastian remained in the reception marquee, drinking whiskey.

Meanwhile, inside the pool house, Benedict Templeton-Mancini and his friend Jack Welling were enjoying some sexual activity. Earlier, two waitresses had caught the eye of the two friends and arranged to meet them at the pool house.

The waitresses were much older than Jack and Benedict. Stripping off, both women flaunted their naked bodies. Jack stripped and joined the two women cavorting amongst the blue-striped cushions on the wicker beds. The tall waitress threw packets of condoms onto a glass wicker table.

Benedict sat motionless in the opposite wicker chair watching the orgy. One of the women called Claudette walked over to Benedict and tried to unbuckle his belt, but Benedict shoved her away.

"My wallet is in the other pocket," Benedict said. Remaining clothed in his tuxedo, he unfastened his tie and continued to watch the show.

"Man, are you going to join us?" Jack asked.

"Doesn't do anything for me." Benedict relaxed back into his chair.

"You gay?" Claudette said, continuing to frolic with Jack.

"Beer, sirs?" the butler broke in, offering Benedict a silver tray.

"Jack doesn't want beer, he's in the middle of his performance." Benedict grinned, accepting the drinks. "But he could do with some more rubbers."

****

Allison performed four songs and bowed to her audience with the band. The original wedding musicians replaced Templeton.

"Promise me, no songs of mine!" Allison said to the guys adjusting their instruments.

"You got it, Miss Alice!" smiled the wedding singer. Counting five, the band began to play tracks from the seventies.

Following her former bandmates, Allison bumped into Charles Medley-Garrett. "Glass of champagne? Keep you young."

“Then you must be a teenager,” Allison laughed, “Yes, please.”

The theatre director’s piercing blue eyes cut into her.

“Nice tux. Steal it from Buckingham?”

Charles grinned. “My English accent?”

“Belinda thinks you are King Arthur,” she sniggered.

“In a past life, maybe I was. Your friend is something. Seemed a lot smarter on TV.”

“I don’t watch TV,” she said.

“I’d have loved to have seen the four of you all together.”

Allison looked at the floor and thought of Fay.

“Sorry if it still upsets you.” Charles placed his huge hand upon Allison’s shoulder.

Electricity ran into her body and nearly blew her over.

“Alice, would you like to dance?”

“With you?” she grinned, resting her champagne glass on a table. “Shall we…”

Walking onto the dance floor, Allison gripped onto Charles, swaying against the rhythm of the soft, calming music. She felt like Cinderella. This was a different feeling than she had with Romano. Feeling the tenderness from his body, she sighed.

Charles cleared his throat. “Been a long time since I danced.”

“Sorry about your wife.” Allison stared into his handsome features.

Placing his hand on her uncovered back, Allison shuddered. “I’m sorry, backless dresses are awkward for a gentleman,” he whispered.

“Not the best design,” she said. “When do you fly back?”

“Tomorrow.”

“Sebastian remains in New York until April, correct?”

“Correct.”

Allison’s stomach was in knots. The music ended, and Allison pulled away and applauded. Reaching for her hand, Charles kissed it.

“Thank you,” Charles gazed into her soft brown eyes and time had stopped.

A voice interrupted, “Father, our car has arrived.”

Nathaniel and Angel appeared. “I will escort them out, Mom!” Nathaniel grinned.

“Thank you, Angel, Charles, for attending.”

Charles nodded and walked away with Angel and Nathaniel into the darkness.

A familiar voice sounded from behind. “I know that look, Alice.”

“Stephen!”

Stephen-Paul Golding stood by her side. “Is it love?”

"Is what love?" Allison snapped.

"The Englishman."

"Romano is my love."

"I haven't seen him all night."

"I was busy onstage."

"You could always step off." Stephen chuckled.

"It's my job."

"Oh my God! You danced with King Arthur?" Belinda intruded. "Hey, Stephen," she kissed him on the cheek.

"Belinda," Stephen replied lifting his head from the kiss.

Allison remained silent. Lucinda, Helen, and Adele came bounding across the flashing psychedelic lights.

"Wow, what's he like?" Lucinda asked.

"My time to disappear," said Stephen.

Allison grabbed his arm. "Oh no, you're staying."

"Do I have to?" Stephen moaned, terrified.

Belinda grabbed his other arm. "Yes!"

"Well, Nathaniel, I think he's falling in love with Angel. The Medley-Garretts are flying back to London tomorrow." Allison still held onto Stephen.

"What's he like?" Helen said, gripping her drink.

"English," Allison replied. "Sebastian's boss!"

Stephen found his exit to escape and disappeared into the crowd of people dancing. Allison soon found an adequate excuse to remove herself from her friends and walked alone up to the main house.

Ordering a tea, she lounged in the sitting room when Romano burst in and shattered the peace.

"Where were you, another award ceremony?"

"Singing," she said, removing her black suede stilettos.

"Come here, baby. Let me do your feet."

Simons carried in a china tea set and placed it down on the walnut table. "Miss Alice, would you like me to pour?"

"No, thank you."

"Madam." Simons bowed and removed himself from the sitting room.

Romano rubbed Allison's feet.

"Sorry I wasn't with you tonight. It's been hectic!" Romano spoke.

"I was performing with Templeton, catching up with the guys. I miss them, but not the music."

"Belinda's doing my head in with Seb's boss."

"We danced. He explained Sebastian will be back in London next April."

"Six months in New York?" Romano huffed.

"Is Maria..."

"Both in bed!" Romano laughed removing his shoes.

"The kids?"

"Seb and Sarah-Jane have retired." Romano grinned, removing his tie. "You know what they'll be doing!"

"Romano, it's 1:30." Allison said.

"My watch stopped."

"I'll buy you another one."

The couple laughed and cuddled up to one another. The wedding reception had been a success. At last, they were both alone in the depths of their beloved sitting room. Allison's had proven once again to be a devoted mother and wife – perfect.

CHAPTER 4

Castrum Place - Rye - New York

15th September 2005

A skeletal figure rested upon arranged pillows, asleep. Paul Freidman placed himself into a nursing chair. Gripping onto the bone and loose skin, he held her fading hand.

"Until death," he whispered.

Paul, sixty-nine, still retained his youthful looks even though his hair and imperial beard were now pure white.

"Don't leave me, Miranda."

Miranda Freidman laid unconscious. In January 2005, she was diagnosed with pancreatic cancer. The disease had overcome her frail body at speed, spreading into her liver, lungs, and brain.

Paul was devastated and heartbroken at the effects it had caused his wife. He tried on several occasions to pay good money for new treatments, but the treatments failed.

Looking up at the ceiling, he breathed while tears trickled down his face. Remaining still, he gripped even harder onto Miranda's skeletal hand. She opened her eyes.

"Miranda?" Paul kissed her pale, lifeless face.

Her grip loosened. She was gone. Paul stood up and gripped Miranda's shoulders, pulling her forward from the pillows, hugging her while he rocked their bodies together.

Paul bellowed in pain. He finally laid Miranda back down onto the pillows and covered her face with a gold crest scarf.

The door opened. Doctor Latimer stepped in and removed his stethoscope.

“You’re too late,” Paul said.

“Mr Freidman, we did everything we could. I will arrange with the undertakers to remove…”

“I would like my wife to remain here,” Paul scowled.

“By law, an autopsy…”

Paul scrambled toward the middle-aged doctor. “I never cared about the law before. Why start now?”

Miles Peterson stormed into the bedroom and gripped Paul, restraining his arms, he softly said, “Paul, let the man do his job. Miranda is gone!”

“Gone?” Paul touched the limp body. “She’s right here.”

***

Montrose Gatehouse III - Mayfair - London

18th October 2005

“Mother, can you help me find my book?” an impeccable male English accent sounded from the patio door.

Hillary dropped her full lotus position and plummeted onto the yoga mat. “Darling, I believe your English book is in my office. On the desk!” she yelled.

“Found it!” he yelled back.

Tobias picked up his English book. He noticed his mother's laptop was open and understood that she may be busy today.

Hillary, now dressed in a white robe, said, "Eggs?"

"Please," he said, taking his seat at the white island.

"How is school, Tobias?" She broke two eggs on the side of a frying pan.

"I'm glad to have taken an extra year before university, that extra A Level will make the difference."

Eighteen-year-old Tobias's aim was law school, but he needed that extra qualification to maintain his acceptance. So, he endured an extra year on a foundation course at St Wilfred's College.

Tobias attended a private school in London from the age of four. He grew into a very intelligent young man and remained close to his friends, who had now departed to university.

The handsome mixed-raced male captured the attention of the opposite sex. Every female wanted to devour him. His beautiful white smile and huge dark brown eyes apprehended every aspect of sexual spice within the male. Unfortunately for the females of the world, he preferred men.

Hillary understood that her son preferred the same sex and encouraged him not to hide it. Being a sex therapist,

Hillary greatly advised her son and became happy when he lost his virginity at the age of seventeen to Tristan, his short-term boyfriend.

Eating his eggs, Tobias said, “Mother, are you in conferences today?”

Hillary looked up with her piercing blue eyes and her light American accent answered, “Yes, all day.”

“I just noticed your laptop was open.”

“You did what? What did you see on—”

The answering machine beeped. “Hi, Stella. It’s Miles. I’m in London. Call me on this number.”

“Who’s Miles, mom?” Tobias asked.

Hillary became deadly pale and collapsed on the kitchen floor. “They found me!”

***

Pullman House - Pennsylvania

30th October 2005 - 7.00 p.m.

Working on approving regulations and supporting agendas, Jake leaned back into his executive black leather desk chair. Placing both arms behind his neck, he stretched.

A knock sounded. Jake removed himself from his seat. Opening the heavy door, he was greeted by his smiling daughter.

“Daddy, may I come in?”

"I don't know. Can you?" he scooped her up and brought her inside.

Nine-year-old Fay-Elizabeth Pullman loved her father and constantly wanted to sit with him. Placing his blonde-haired daughter into an armchair, he sat across from her.

"Good day at school?" he said.

Fay nodded. "Mummy is different today!" she exclaimed, swinging her legs against the leather chair.

"Different?" Jake asked.

"Mummy!" Fay giggled, looking over her father's shoulder.

Turning around, Jake gasped, "Your hair!"

"Yeah, do you like it?" Helen said, walking into the office. She was wearing a navy-blue trouser suit, which captured her curves and shapely legs.

"It reminds me of the first day we met in my office." Jake kissed her on the lips and smudged her makeup.

"I just can't keep pace with the grey. Dark hair shows every little white strand!" she laughed, reapplying her lipstick.

Jake ran his fingers through his styled dark greying hair. "Yes, my grey is not too bad!" he laughed.

"I am older than you," she reminded him.

"Have I got grey?" Fay piped up.

"No, darling, you have years yet," Helen laughed.

The nanny Mrs Buckley walked into the office and knocked on the doorframe. "Bedtime, Miss Fay."

Fay moaned in despair, "Do I have to?"

"Yes, darling, I will come to tuck you in. Shall we read *Harry the Hairless Werewolf*?"

"That's my favourite!" Fay grinned in delight.

Mrs Buckley held out her hand as Jake lifted his little princess from the leather button chair. Blowing a huge raspberry on her rosy cheek, Fay giggled and kicked her feet. Eventually reaching the oak flooring, she ran towards Mrs Buckley, waving goodnight to her father.

"You are a great dad!" Helen smiled in contentment.

"You are a good mom!" Jake raised his eyebrows.

Jake ordered two coffees to be taken into the sitting room while he and Helen cleared his office.

Strolling hand in hand into the distinguished sitting room, Helen and Jake positioned themselves in front of the antique fireplace. Above the mantelpiece hung a huge oil portrait of WJ Pullman.

WJ Pullman had passed away a few years before, in August 2003. He was eighty-three years old and died from a stroke. Jake and Helen were devastated by their loss and WJ rested next to his beloved wife in the family tomb.

Jake gripped his Lex University mug of steaming coffee and smiled at Helen sitting across from him.

"Blonde again," he spoke. "Are you Helen Pullman or Helen of Troy?"

"You never were good at pillow talk," she replied, kicking off her blue stilettos and positioning her feet on the suede cream sofa.

Jake coughed. "I have to travel to London."

"Not work. Freidman?"

"Yes, with Miles," he answered.

"You've found her…Stella."

"Miles is already in London." Jake said, sipping his coffee and looking into the unlit fire. "She changed her name."

Helen knew by the expression on Jake's face that it was history repeating itself, all because of one man.

"When do you leave?" she muttered into her mug.

"In a couple of days…I'm taking Clive." Jake answered, crossing his legs.

"Chartered flight?"

"English Airlines. Clive's weapons will have to be declared before we even reach the airport," Jake sighed.

"Bodyguards…" Helen frowned.

"I'll need one."

***

Liberty House Hotel - Central London

1st November 2005

A black London cab pulled up outside the glass double doors of the supreme entrance. A doorman wearing a grey top hat and silver-braided San Marino overcoat stepped out and opened the rear passenger door.

Clive Goodison removed himself from the rear seat while Jake followed from behind. The doorman ordered two porters to remove the guest's luggage from the trunk of the cab and load it onto brass trolleys. Both men nodded and strolled into the five-star hotel.

A large reception desk hosted three uniformed clerks.

"Good morning, sir..." A beautiful, mid-height, dark-haired clerk smiled.

"Check in, please." Jake placed two sets of passports on the marbled counter.

"Senator Pullman?" the female clerk replied, looking at her computer screen.

"Mr will do fine," Jake replied.

"Sorry, Mr Pullman."

Once Jake and Clive had checked in, both entered the glass lift with a porter and shown to their penthouse suite on the top floor. Opening the door, Jake and Clive stepped into the designer suite.

"Wow!" Clive said.

"Yeah, yeah," Jake replied, walking over towards a set of double glass doors.

"A balcony?" Clive exclaimed. "I can see the Tower of London!"

"Good, we can lock up Freidman!"

"Where am I, boss?" Clive asked, opening the bedroom doors.

"There are four rooms, pick one," Jake replied, walking into the kitchen area. "This milk had better not be expired."

"So, we're all supplied up," Clive said, observing a mini fridge.

"Help yourself. All charges go on my credit card," Jake said.

"Mr Peterson, he is staying in this hotel?" Clive enquired.

"Fifth floor."

Jake removed his black cashmere long winter coat and sported his typical navy-blue suit and coordinating tie. A knock at the door grabbed his attention. Clive pulled his gun from his holster, flicked the safety off, and opened the door.

"Damn it, Miles! You could have warned me you were coming," Clive said, lowering his weapon.

"Room service," he laughed.

Miles removed his black cashmere long jacket and whistled. "Some view."

"We had some sexy women here, but they all left when they heard you were coming." Clive laughed.

"Good to see you, Jake." Miles ignored Clive's joke.

"Coffee?" Jake said.

"Something a bit stronger," Miles said, pointing to the wine cabinet.

"Black, then. Clive?"

"Just juice," Clive said, joining Miles on the designer mustard corner sofa. "I'm on the clock."

Jake handed Miles a glass of merlot. "So, Miles, you think the woman in Mayfair is Stella?"

"Who else?" he said, lowering his glass.

"How do you know?"

"She doesn't venture out much, but I have managed to track her," Miles grinned, staring at Jake and Clive.

"I just don't get it. If she doesn't go out much…"

"I follow her kid," Miles interrupted, rubbing his upper lip.

Jake froze. "A kid?"

"Tobias Jonah, eighteen…" Miles said.

"Freidman's?"

"No, I think he's mine!" Miles stepped in.

“You slept with her!” Jake announced.

“She is the only woman I have ever loved. Of course, I slept with her,” Miles jerked forward.

“You think this kid is yours?” Jake snatched his glass of whiskey and drunk a mouthful.

“Yes, but I can’t get near the house! The street is sealed off with security gates.”

“Security gates?” Jake muffled into his glass. “Who’s her neighbour, the president?”

“Templeton-Mancini.”

“At least presidents have been shot. Nobody messes with the Mancinis.”

Clive cut in, “Sebastian!”

“Yep, but he’s living in New York now. He’s on Broadway again.”

“So, what’s the plan?” Jake cut in.

“You mean how do we speak to Stella?” Miles answered.

“Yeah!” Clive dived in.

Miles paused. “I have her business number and left several messages on her voicemail. She works as a sex therapist…”

“She’s not looking at me naked,” Clive interrupted.

“Shut up, Clive,” Jake said.

“She has a home office,” Miles added.

“Right! In the morning, Clive can make an appointment,” Jake announced. “An emergency.”

“A sexual emergency?” Clive looked up and glared at Miles and Jake. “Like what?”

“Unzip your pants and we will work it out!”

***

Montrose Gatehouse III - Mayfair - London

2nd November 2005 - 9.00 a.m.

Hillary walked into her office on a typical dull November morning. Opening her laptop, she received one new message: “Is it possible to book an emergency appointment? Mr Singleton.”

Hilary opened her diary and checked her appointments. Yes, it was a clear day. Deciding to arrange the appointment for 11:00 a.m., she emailed the client back. At £150/per hour, she couldn’t refuse the work.

Stepping into her kitchen Hilary could smell the aroma from her percolator. She smiled when she heard a ping from her laptop next door. Her morning session had been accepted. The next job after her coffee was to prepare notes for the 11:00 a.m. therapy session.

***

Liberty House Hotel - Central London

2nd November 2005 - 10.45 a.m.

Miles arranged his laptop on the dining table, placing a notebook with questions and answers by the side of the computer for Clive to reference. Clive rehearsed his opening speech and Jake awarded him a thumbs up.

"Remember, don't give it away," Miles said.

Clive nodded while sitting down at the table. Miles entered his username and password and began to dial.

The connection clicked. A soft American accent sounded from the laptop.

"Hi, my name is Hillary Jonah. I am here to help with any of your sexual problems."

Clive interrupted with his English accent, "Hi, my name is Clifford Singleton and I need help."

"Hi, Clifford. Payment is after the session, okay? You can wire the money from my invoice."

"Not a problem." Clive gulped.

"Please continue," Hillary said, crossing her arms.

Reading his script, Clive explained his difficulties in bed, blushing even more while his arousal was killing him under the table.

Hillary continued to advise him on lubrication and foreplay.

“Is it possible to have a one-to-one session? I can’t do this onscreen,” he said.

“I’m sorry, I only do it online,” Hillary said, taking notes.

“I need to see the lubrications. Do you have illustrations or something like that?” Clive insisted.

Hillary began to feel uncomfortable.

“How do I know you’re not a fraud?” Clive asked.

“I am not a fraud! I guarantee I have qualifications, Mr Singleton,” Hillary announced.

“I am not a pervert…I need help! My wife is going to leave me, and I love her so much. It’s breaking my heart!” Clive pretended to cry.

“Please don’t cry.” Hillary lowered her notebook.

“I’m desperate.” Clive continued to weep.

Jake and Miles looked at one another.

“Come and see me within the next hour. My address is Montrose Gatehouse III, Mayfair. I’ll buzz you in.”

“Thank you. Thank you…” Clive sniffled as the connection clicked off.

Cheering and clapping echoed throughout the elegant suite.

“You, my man, are the best.” Miles high-fived Clive.

“That performance was better than Sebastian Templeton-Mancini,” Jake laughed.

Clive stood up from his seat and announced, "I need to change my pants!"

***

Montrose Gatehouse III - Mayfair - London - 2nd November 2005 - 11.55 a.m.

The grim darkness of nimbostratus clouds submerged the City of London. Hillary was pacing around her floral office when she saw herself in the window's reflection, an ageing woman with long auburn-coloured hair tied into a bun. Breaking her thoughts, the gate buzzer alerted the professional woman back down to the planet Earth.

Never checking the camera, Hillary pressed the open button. Clive positioned himself, staring at the ugly black door knocker. With his hands in his coat pockets, he whistled. Jake and Miles crouched, out of view.

The door opened.

"Clifford?" Hillary said. "Please, come in."

Clive stepped inside as Miles appeared. The horror on Hillary's face slaughtered her pretty features.

Miles yelled, "Baby, Freidman's not here! He thinks you're dead!"

Hillary gasped, "Senator Pullman!"

"Jake! Can we come in, Stella?" Jake looked behind making sure that the coast was clear.

Hillary remained quiet while tears trickled down her beautiful face. She guided the three males towards her sitting room. Miles stopped and grabbed her into his muscular arms as she closed the entrance door. She started sobbing into his chest.

Miles breathed a sigh of relief: she was his at last. Jake turned around and witnessed the scene between the old lovers. "I'll make the drinks," he said, walking towards the kitchen.

"Before we all sit down, may I take you somewhere more private?" Miles whispered into her sweet-smelling hair.

Hillary pointed towards her office door. They walked together and hugged. She sniffled. Sitting Hillary down on a soft two-seater red fabric sofa, Miles pulled the white leather desk chair from beneath Hillary's desk and wheeled it opposite the sobbing female. He took his place, handing her a tissue from an isolated box on top of her desk. He swamped the desk chair with his huge, toned body.

"What happened, baby?" he asked.

"He tried to kill me…" she said in-between sobs.

"Freidman! He did four crew members," he announced, standing from his chair, and removing his long cashmere jacket.

Hillary noticed his toned figure and continued to watch the male of worth.

Sitting back down, he said, "So how did you survive?"

Hillary snapped herself out of it. "I was a mess, rejected, unloved…Paul was having an affair. He only screwed me to shut me up, but you know all of that!" Hillary continued to look directly at Miles. "I managed to sneak forty million dollars from under his nose, stashed it in an offshore bank account."

Miles punched his left hand. "Jonathan Greatly, I knew it. I never trusted that bastard."

"Every transfer, a million dollars went missing. Jon cooked the books!"

"Why charter a cruise in the Caribbean?" Miles asked, puzzled.

"That was my way out. I had planned to fall overboard, paid a fishing boat to rescue me, but Paul's crew members got to me first. They tried to strangle me. Paul's orders." Hillary stopped and took a slow deep breath before continuing. "I played dead when I realised, they were trying to kill me and then they threw me overboard."

"How did you…?" Miles was speechless.

"The fisherman I paid never stopped looking for me," she sighed. "They found me drifting near a coral reef. I changed into fresh clothing when I returned to shore. My car was waiting with my luggage."

"How did you leave the country?"

"While Paul was screwing his mistress, Jonathan had located me an apartment in Hackney, London, for £1.17 million. Jon already taught me how to falsify the forms. Some cheap lipstick and a haircut and Hillary Jonah was born. New photograph, new birth certificate, new passport. After the background check, I flew straight to the UK."

"Is he mine?"

Hillary looked down at her stomach. "Yes."

"My God," Miles said. "I have a son!"

"I hired a nanny while I studied for my degree as a therapist."

"Does he ask about his father?" Miles asked.

"No, we never talk about it. My life back then was a mess. I was on the road to self-destruction…"

"Why a sex therapist?" Miles asked, leaning in, and grabbing Hillary's shaking hand.

"I was a sex addict. Thought I could turn a hobby into a career."

"How do you feel about me now?" Miles sprang the question.

"I'm still talking, aren't I?"

"What about Tobias? He should meet his father."

"But I live here in London, you in New York. Stella Jane Bing is dead."

"I have unfinished business with Freidman. Once he's out of the way, we'll be a family again. I swear."

"You'd move to London for me?"

"I'd move to hell. Marry me?"

***

Jake tapped at the office door. "Coffee's ready!"

"Coming through," replied Miles, admiring his new fiancée. "Ready to meet Jake and Clive?"

Hillary nodded and stood up, placing her damp tissue into a red floral bin. "I need to grab another one!" she said, reaching for the box.

Miles and Hilary strolled out of the office into the sitting room. Hillary's eyes were bloodshot, and her cheeks were burning red.

"Sorry about my appearance…I'm not used to having guests!" she said.

"I hope you like instant," Jake said. "I think I broke your coffee machine."

Placing three sugar lumps and a handful of milk into his coffee, Clive spoke, "I'm sorry to mislead you, but it was the only way we could get in."

"I'm glad you did," she smiled, glancing at Miles.

"I'm Clive, not Clifford. Pullman's bodyguard."

Hillary laughed, "I still have to charge you for the session."

Jake cut in, "Stella!"

Hillary blurted, "Stella is dead!"

Jake apologized. "Are all your documentation in the name of Hillary Jonah?"

"Yes. Stella Jane was announced dead after seven years," Miles said.

"Okay, Hillary, Freidman believes you are dead. It will remain that way. He is currently being watched by the authorities. Only a matter of time before he's caught. The logistics side is withholding his goods due to aggressive custom checks. Time is money, and he's out," Jake announced.

"Why tell me this?" Hillary said.

"I want to tell you before the TV does," Jake blew the steam from his coffee.

Miles looked at Hillary. "You okay with it?"

"Dying is awfully complicated."

CHAPTER 5

TWC - Paris - 4th November 2005

A powerful shot exploded across the indoor tennis court. Jas Olsson raised his racket and swung it from his right hip. Sending the ball down the middle line, Benedict Templeton-Mancini served an ace shot: game, set, and match.

Dropping to his knees, Mancini puffed with exhaustion. Spectators applauded. Eighteen-year-old Benedict ran over to the net and greeted Olsson with a handshake.

Collecting his belongings and picking up his rackets, Benedict waved to Sebastian Dupont sitting in the VIP box with Oliver. Leaving the court, Benedict waved to the crowd and disappeared into a tunnel. Paris officials walked alongside until he reached the dressing rooms.

Matty Barker was chatting to Benedict's lover Lee S. Marconi. Mancini and Marconi were always the number one players to watch: rivals on court, lovers in the bedroom.

Hot and sweaty, Benedict winked at Lee and fist-bumped Matty. Jas Olsson followed behind with Paris officials and disappeared into another changing room. Matt allowed Lee into the dressing room with Benedict, under clearance.

Walking into the blue-tiled expanse area, two double shower cubicles awaited Benedict. Lee assisted with the undressing and placed himself on a bench, while Benedict entered the steaming shower.

Benedict shouted above the sound of running water, "I wish you'd come in!"

Lee, who had already showered from an earlier match, laughed. "No, you can have me later!"

A mumbling echoed from the cubicle.

Smelling of citrus, Benedict walked out of the shower, naked, displaying his olive-toned body. Brushing his dripping shoulder-length hair back, he grabbed a blue towel from the rack and tied it around his waist.

"Round four next!" Benedict sighed, grabbing yet another towel from a hook.

"I'll see you in the final again," scoffed Lee. "Maybe you'll even win this time."

"Willerby Houghton is climbing the ranks!"

"Match fixing," responded Lee, messing with his mobile.

"I have to go for a drug test in ten minutes," Benedict said, drying himself harshly.

"See you tonight, Room 15."

"Room 15." Benedict let his towel fall and grabbed Lee into a passionate kiss. Lee disappeared from the dressing room. Six polished wooden benches and metal hooks lay abandoned while another bench displayed a clothing bag, with a leather jacket hung on a peg.

An official came into the changing room while Benedict was tying his trainers. Standing at six-foot-two, he pulled on his leather jacket over his white t-shirt and blue jeans.

Pinning his hair into a ponytail, he collected his racket and clothing bag. Benedict followed the official to the test centre.

After giving a clear blood and urine sample, Benedict was cleared to leave the arena. Matty walked alongside Benedict with his coaches, Marlow Slyton and Geoff Glowburg. Sebastian and Oliver Dupont waited inside the VIP area and congregated with other dignitaries.

A silver SUV waited outside the exit door. Matty checked for clearance with the arena security and escorted Benedict, Sebastian, and Oliver to the seven-seater vehicle. Marlow and Geoff followed behind.

Pulling away from the spectacular blue covered building, crowds of fans waved at Benedict. Sebastian forced his head down. "Why is this car not privacy protected?"

"This is the only one we could hire," Marlow said from the rear.

"No Mercedes?" Sebastian answered.

"If you want a Mercedes, we're passing a dealership on the way," Marlow responded.

"I shall arrange something more private. This is Benedict Templeton-Mancini we are transporting," Sebastian replied, raising his head.

"I thought you retired," Marlow mumbled.

"When I need to be, darling!"

Oliver grinned, "I love this vacation."

Pulling up to the 5-star Fabuleux Hotel. Sebastian said, "At least the hotel is stylish."

Oliver laughed. "You have the penthouse suite!"

Sebastian huffed.

Removing himself from the middle seat of the SUV, Benedict strode into the hotel lobby. The Baroque style introduced several shimmering mirrors, chandeliers, and an open plan carbon black and copper lounge. After organising their dinner arrangements with Sebastian and Oliver, Benedict and Matty headed towards a mirrored elevator.

"Ben, please be advised that you cannot go to Lee's room. I must have a connecting door for security," Matty responded, walking into the elevator.

"I forgot!"

"Ring his room number and he comes to you, okay?" Matty grinned, selecting button number 4.

Benedict raised his thumb in approval. Carrying all his sports bags, he stumbled out of the elevator with his bodyguard. Walking to rooms 47 & 49, Matty swiped his key card in the door device, Benedict entered his suite.

Dropping his bags onto the vermilion carpet, he paced towards the fridge, selected an orange juice, and swallowed.

Matty opened the partition door and notified Benedict. "6:50, okay?"

"You got it!" grinned Benedict, dialling a number on his mobile. Matty closed his door and continued with his shower plan.

Benedict's phone connected the call. "Lee, you have to stay in my room tonight."

"Okay," a whispering mellow voice sounded. "Security?"

"You got it. Room 47."

"10:30. See you there." The mobile rang off.

Benedict collected his soiled sports clothing and threw them into Marlow's team laundry bag. Opening the door, he placed them outside his luxury suite. Remaining calm, he walked into his room and was about to close the door when Willerby Houghton burst in.

Walking around Benedict's elegant sitting room of reds, yellows, and umber, the American whistled, placing himself onto the fabric red sofa.

"You're a king, Ben!"

"What the hell do you want, Will?"

Willerby looked around the room and sprawled his size nine sneakers onto the coffee table. “Well, that depends on you!”

Benedict towered over the tennis player and cracked his knuckles.

“I need you to lose the next match.”

“As long as my opponent loses first.”

“Or the world will find out about Shirley Templeton-Mancini and lover boy.”

Benedict strolled over to his breakfast bar in the kitchenette area. Taking his seat on a black leather stool, he grunted. “The world, huh?”

“Yeah, and if you like living in it, I suggest you play ball.” Willerby smirked, playing with the corner of the sofa’s headrest.

“Not with you!” Benedict growled.

“I’m just thinking about your popularity. Mancini, Marconi. You know how it goes... unless you want to pay me off. Let’s start the bidding at one million dollars.”

“Blackmail?” Benedict laughed.

The partition door slowly opened, and Matty shovelled quietly in his grey jogging bottoms and bare feet, pointing his Glock 19.

“You Mancinis are….” Willerby stopped in mid-sentence. He felt the barrel on the back of his head.

"On the floor now!" yelled Matty, pushing Willerby forward.

Stretched out on his stomach, holding both hands up, Willerby peed himself. Matty frisked him while still pointing the gun at the back of his head.

"Get up!" Matty yelled.

Willerby slowly pulled himself up and looked down at his wet patch staining his jeans. Still holding both hands up, he began to shake.

"Blackmail doesn't become you, little boy."

Willerby shook his head and ran out of the room.

****

Fabuleux Hotel - Paris - 4th November 2005 - 7.00 p.m.

Dressed to perfection, Sebastian Dupont lounged against his high back chair engraved with gold and copper swirls. Wearing a black pinstriped suit and red cravat, Sebastian took in the atmosphere.

Oliver Dupont sipped his flute of *Pinot Noir*, glancing at the opposite table. Benedict, wearing his open neck black dress shirt and grey suit, anticipated the garçon placing him at the table. Matty followed.

Marlow and Geoff shortly made themselves present in their black dress shirts and grey suits.

Sebastian said, "Marlow! Do tell me what the motif on your suit is."

Benedict looked down at his suit handkerchief pocket and observed a gladiator holding the world.

"The Academy of Chaquen. We pride ourselves with winning champions."

"Oh, I see. Your sponsors, Inex..." Sebastian enquired.

"The pink double-cross logo is on our players' equipment and clothing." Marlow continued, accepting his menu.

"Geoff, what team is sitting behind us?" Oliver stepped in.

"Oh, Marden's sponsors are Ogho."

"Are they any good?" enquired Oliver, interested in Geoff's response.

"They tend to take stage three players. We, the Academy, take stage six."

****

Room 22 - Fabuleux Hotel - Paris

5th November 2005 - 1.00 a.m.

Stretch out under a yellow and red striped duvet, Willerby Houghton tossed and turned, frightened by a near-death experience. The twenty-six-year-old tennis player was futile in qualifying for the quarterfinals.

Blackmailing and match fixing earned him the cash and a ranking. His parents, investment bankers, supported him financially. In his time, he tried to date Ann Templeton-

Miller but failed miserably when David La-Mount-Martinez punched him in Discis night club. He despised the Mancinis, especially Benedict. Not realising that his bodyguards were armed, he had to back off or die.

Falling back into a deep sleep, his body fell still. A creaking door released bright light from the passageway as a tall figure crawled into the room.

Willerby's bare arm hung over the tip of the duvet as he laid on his back. The stranger pulled out a syringe, jammed it into Willerby's forearm, and pushed the plunger. The dark figure opened the door and disappeared.

The next morning, Willerby felt more tired than usual. Striding towards the bathroom, he misplaced his footing and fell over, slamming his serving hand into the dresser.

"Damn!"

****

Victoire Arena - 5th November 2005 - 1.30 p.m.

Lee S. Marconi walked out onto the main arena court, waving to his fans. Carrying his equipment, he placed himself on the metal seats and unzipped his blue hoodie. Following him, Willerby Houghton wore his typical white-and-yellow zigzag stripe.

Refusing to look at his opponent, Willerby walked over to the seats positioned left of the umpire. Wiping his racket with his towel, Willerby felt ill. Trying to reach the baseline to warm up nearly killed him.

Sebastian and Oliver Dupont relaxed in the VIP box. Sebastian sported a white tailored jacket, black cravat, trousers, and a straw boater. Oliver commented on his English design.

"My dear Oliver, tennis is an Englishman's game. At least my man I do dress for the part."

Lee S. Marconi impressed Sebastian with his medium length blonde hair, sparkling blue eyes and sun-kissed tan.

Standing at six-foot-one, his toned body began make Sebastian hot under the collar. "I love Ben's boyfriend," he whispered to Oliver.

Oliver laughed. "Calm down, dear husband!"

Lee won the toss and within his first shots Lee had served three aces, the game was already at forty-love. Willerby was off-balance and within an hour, the first set was won by Marconi 6-0.

Sebastian smiled. "I love this match; it is quite exciting."

"Would be more exciting if Houghton hit the ball." Oliver replied.

After a five-minute break, Marconi and Houghton returned to the court. Houghton served and hit the net twice, 15-love. The umpire sounded: double fault. Lee shrugged his shoulders and looked at his coach.

The match ended 3-0. Lee waved to the crowd and collected his rackets and bags, pacing from the scene, peeved that he had not achieved a battle. Easy wins didn't please him.

Willerby threw his racket bag down on the dressing room floor and vomited.

His coach stormed in. "What the hell happened?"

"Don't talk to me. I felt like crap. Must be the flu!"

"Your practise session this morning was a disgrace."

"Look!" Willerby lifted his right hand.

"What happened to you, street fight?"

"With my dresser. I'm ruined," he sighed, dropping down onto a bench.

"We'll get you a sports physician. Rehab."

"I don't need rehab. I need a shower."

The coach disappeared from the dressing room, and Willerby showered in agony.

Drying himself off, Willerby dressed into his jeans and a black t-shirt. Grabbing his gear, he followed an official to the test centre.

The clinician handed a glass sample bottle to Willerby. He disappeared into a cubicle and relieved himself. Screwing the lid on the container, he washed his hands and returned it to an official sitting at a desk. The doctors took his blood, and Willerby signed the paperwork.

The rapid urine drug test showed traces of an illegal substance. Willerby and his team had to wait for the full outcome when the urine and blood test results returned from the lab.

The test showed orange. Willerby was shocked. His coach was even more horrified by the result and instructed Willerby to remain in his room for the next couple of days.

The drugs test came back and revealed cocaine. Willerby Houghton received a tennis ban for two years and his coach dropped him from the team permanently.

Mancini and Marconi were in the semi-finals. Sebastian Dupont was elated – everything had worked out perfectly.

CHAPTER 6

Millers - Sphere Films Studio - Los Angeles

15th February 2006.

Rupert Templeton-Mancini carried his folder and headphones. Quickly pacing alongside the parked trailers, he cursed under his breath, "I'm going to beat him to a pulp!"

Screaming and shrieking erupted outside studio six. Opening the lavish motorhome door, Rupert pushed his way in, slamming the door behind him. Slouching on a custom-made Italian sofa, Nathaniel Templeton-Mancini placed each forefinger into his ears. Leaning over a double electric recliner, leading actress Crystal Sylvia screamed.

"What the hell!" shouted Rupert, storming into the living area.

"Tape her mouth up!" Nathaniel yelled.

"Crystal! Crystal!" Rupert shouted.

Sobbing, Sylvia collapsed into a heap on the brown carpet. Pointing at Nathaniel, she whimpered, "He won't have sex with me!"

"What?" Rupert yelled.

"He does it with everyone else," she sobbed. "Except me!"

Rupert glared at his brother trying to ignore the commotion. "I don't believe this!" Rupert said, throwing his headphones onto the marble table. Grabbing the distraught actress up from the floor, he dragged her towards the bedroom.

The eye-catching room featured a king-sized bed with a plasma TV and mirrored ceiling-to-floor wall tiles. Rupert pushed the actress onto the bed. Pointing at her, he snarled. "Calm down and stay in here!"

Closing the door, he paced over to Nathaniel and punched him in the chest.

"Ouch! That hurt," Nathaniel said, pulling his fingers out of his ears.

"What's going off?" Rupert growled.

"She caught me romping with Cheryl."

"Cheryl, your stylist?" Rupert said, falling back against the sofa headrest.

"It was a quicky," Nathaniel replied, leaning back with his brother.

"Why is she doing one?"

"She's a fruit loop! Beer?"

Rupert facepalmed. Nathaniel removed toned body from the sofa. Walking over to the fridge, he selected two fresh bottles and bit off the caps. Walking back towards his brother, he handed Rupert his drink.

"Nat, I suppose that is why you're wearing just your boxers then?"

"I had to find something quick to wear when fruit loop walked in on me."

"Why is she walking in on you? Lock your trailer door next time." Rupert clinked his bottle against Nathaniel's. "Cheers!"

Both brothers took a long-awaited swig of beer and sighed.

"Why don't you just screw her, Nat?"

"Rup, I can't just screw every woman. I'd never have time to drink." Nathaniel paused. "Anyway, I'm in love!"

Rupert spat his beer onto his jeans. "Who's the victim?"

"Angel Medley-Garrett."

"Sebastian's theatre director's...."

"Daughter," Nathaniel continued to drink his beer.

"She's only nineteen...."

"Fake IDs are cheap. Besides, Dad's six years older than Mom!" Nathaniel scowled.

Rupert was intrigued. "When did you meet her?"

"Bro's wedding reception."

"Are you sleeping with her?"

"No. I'm a gentleman," Nathaniel grinned.

"You're taking your time, then?" Rupert said, confused.

"I want to marry her!"

"Oh my God! So, you are screwing your stylist!"

"Saves me money on hair gel!" Nathaniel said continuing drinking his beer.

Rupert shook his head in disbelief. A cough from behind the brothers got their attention.

"Come and get it, boys!"

Both Templeton-Mancinis looked at one another and groaned.

Rupert instantly stood up and looked at her in disgust. "Get dressed!"

Nathaniel grabbed his mobile and called security. Within minutes, two uniformed security guards burst into the motorhome and apprehended the naked actress. Rupert placed a robe around Crystal while the security guards removed her from Nathaniel's trailer.

Rupert walked over to the table and opened his file. Pulling his mobile phone out of his jeans pocket, he began to ring a number. "Hi, it's Rupert Templeton-Mancini. Regarding Crystal, our company do not tolerate drugs or alcohol on-set. I'm afraid she has been dismissed."

****

Mr Golding's Office - Millers-Sphere Studios Los Angeles - 15th February 2006 - 4.30 p.m.

The dull black-and-white office reflected Stephen-Paul Golding's mood. Now fifty-six, executive producer Golding still controlled operations at Millers-Sphere.

Allison Templeton-Mancini positioned herself into a black leather recliner. Wearing her long dark curling hair in an up-do and a two-piece Sylvester-Montgomery red and black trouser suit, she looked the part as president.

Observing Stephen's office, she noticed a silver photo frame positioned next to his address organiser.

"So, the picture is of me?" She laughed at him.

Stephen sat opposite Allison in a recliner of his own. "Could be."

"How many times? You can't have photographs of me, it's weird!" Allison continued to laugh.

"I love you and always will."

Allison reached out and touched his hand. "You're in my heart as well," she smiled with her intense red lipstick.

"You look more like your mother every day."

"Stephen, you're embarrassing me!"

A knock interrupted the conversation. Twenty-three-year-old Rachel Reen appeared around the door frame saying, "Sorry to interrupt, sir, but Rupert Templeton-Mancini would like a meeting."

"Send him in," Allison said.

Rachel nodded and closed the door. "She's pretty. Where's she from?" Allison asked.

"Rachel replaced Agnes last year, visitor's reception desk. She is good at her job."

"Is her job looking good?" Allison grinned.

"Now, now! She is far too young for me," he said. "Now Rupert, on the other hand…

"Are they dating?"

"Yes," Stephen laughed. "Her father is a camera technician, and the family live in the hills."

"What does her mom do?"

"She died when she was young," Stephen fell silent. "Car accident."

"I am so sorry," Allison whispered.

"Kenneth brought her up on his own. Good guy," Stephen explained.

Allison stared at the black woodside executive units running down one side of the room. Above them domineered low level filing cabinets, also in black.

"Romano and you are so similar, black and white," Allison commented.

Stephen laughed. "Opposites are the same thing in different degrees!"

Rupert burst into the office, not paying any attention while he continued to converse with Rachel. Immediately stopping when he witnessed his mother sitting in the lounge area.

"Mom!"

“Rupert!” Allison replied, holding her petite arms out for her colossal son. Rupert grabbed Allison and lifted her from the floor in an intense hug.

Stephen had to intervene. “Rup, put her down. You’re squeezing the life out of her.”

“Sorry, Mom!” he said, lowering her onto the white herringbone rug.

Rupert positioned his place on the leather sofa. “When did you arrive in town?”

“Today. I’m residing with Belinda for the next couple of nights.” Allison replied, fidgeting with her Sylvester briefcase.

“You could have stayed…”

Allison pointed her flame-red fingernail towards Rupert.

“Nathaniel and you are busy people.”

“Aunt Belinda isn’t busy?” Rupert scoffed.

“She can’t even spell it!” laughed Allison.

“Mom, have dinner with us tonight at mine. Nathaniel is coming!”

“Can I bring Belinda?” Allison enquired, still fiddling with her case.

“Yes, Stephen, you as well.”

Stephen looked at Rupert. “Only if Rachel is by your side,” he winked.

Rupert blushed.

Allison said, "It's okay. I know all about it and I want to meet her. Who knows, she may be part of the family one day!"

Rupert lost his composure.

Stephen interrupted Rupert's embarrassment. "So, you wanted to meet?"

"Oh yeah," he stuttered. "I fired Sylvia."

"Why?" Stephen bellowed.

"Cocaine," he replied.

"What happened, she forgot to bring some?" Stephen whistled. "So, we have to pay for the missing scenes."

"I'll have a word with Ray. We can kill her off."

Allison cut in. "Ray?"

"Our script writer," Stephen answered.

Allison looked at Rupert. "What happened?"

Rupert stared at his mother. "I found Crystal screaming at Nat. He wouldn't sleep with her. The woman was covered in…"

"Powder?" Stephen jumped in. "Around her nose?"

"You got it."

Allison observed a serious look. "In Nathaniel's trailer?"

"Correct. I got called to the trailer because she was out of her head."

"Security dealt with it I presume?" Stephen said.

"Yes, I haven't the time for moaning actress's" Rupert huffed.

"I believe your grandpapa once mentioned that line." Smirked Allison.

****

Santiago Del Porto - Bel-Air - Los Angeles

15th February 2006 - 7.00 p.m.

Huge steel security gates opened, and a silver limousine manoeuvred towards the Roman entrance. Rupert waited in the foyer leaning against his black contemporary doors.

The limo stopped. A uniformed driver removed himself from his seat and walked around the car. The front passenger door revealed a blonde-haired male stepping out. Standing at six-foot-three, dressed in a dark grey suit and white shirt, the man nodded at Rupert, who looked like a munchkin next to the handsome giant.

The chauffeur opened the back passenger door and Allison stepped out, holding onto the driver's hand Wearing another stunning knee-length red evening dress, she smiled at her son.

"Rupert!" Allison leaned in and kissed her son's cheek. "Meet Tomas Meier, my new bodyguard.

Rupert stretched his head up and grinned. "What happened to Craig? Did he die?"

“He’ found another body to guard. His own. I think you call it retirement.”

The twenty-nine-year-old bodyguard lived in the Mancini Apartments. Females constantly drooled over him especially the Mancini maids.

Screeching appeared from behind Allison. Belinda, dressed in a white knee-length evening dress, stepped out.

“Rup!” She staggered over to Rupert and planted kiss on his cheek.

“Belinda, you look lovely.” Rupert sized her up.

“Not next to Alice!” Belinda grinned.

Allison scoffed. “Two hours, clothes thrown everywhere…”

“You have to look good when there are stunning men about!” Belinda whispered, looking at Tomas.

“Please, come in…” Rupert guided his mother and Belinda into his home. Turning around, he said to Tomas, “My security, Jono Murrey, and Nat’s security, Jameson Clarke, are downstairs.”

Tomas nodded and dispersed down another set of stairs leading to the ground floor.

Belinda made her entrance and dived towards Nathaniel. “Nat!”

Nathaniel smiled. “Aunt Belinda?”

“Don’t call me Aunt! It makes me feel old!”

“Mom!” Nathaniel leaned down and hugged his mother while Allison kissed his cheek.

After finally releasing her, Allison looked at both of her sons. “I cannot believe that you two still dress the same!”

“We don’t….” Rupert jumped in.

Rupert and Nathaniel stood next to one another dressed in black contour jeans, white dress shirts, and black Sylvester-Montgomery boots.

“What’s the difference?” Allison asked observing her boys.

“Our hair!” Nathaniel piped up. “I don’t like long hair!”

Allison laughed. “Well, it is not exactly short, Nathaniel!”

“Rup’s is much longer than mine, with a side parting.”

“What about your dress code? You both are wearing the same thing!”

Rupert stepped in. “No, my shirt is pearl white. Nat’s is optic white.”

Belinda howled with laughter.

“I need my spectacles!” Allison mumbled.

Suddenly walking into the sitting area Rachel made her presence known. Allison glanced approvingly when she witnessed the most beautiful creature she had seen in a long time.

Rachel stood at five-foot-two, slim, platinum long blonde hair and large blue eyes. Her heart shaped lips smiled at Allison and Belinda. Stunningly wearing an off the shoulder black velvet dinner dress and choker, she made Belinda feel prehistoric.

"Mom, this is Rachel." Rupert introduced his love to his mother. "Rachel, this is…."

"Allison Templeton-Miller, uh, Templeton-Mancini?" she whispered.

Nathaniel laughed "Just Mom!"

Rupert enticed his guests to relax on his soft orange sofas. There were four six seaters with a long oval maple coffee table positioned in the middle. A wooden fruit bowl with extravagant oranges sat in the centre of the table.

Belinda reached over to grip one of the oranges. "My God!" she said, feeling the round object.

Allison burst into laughter. "They're wood, Belinda!"

Belinda quickly placed it back into the bowl. "Max?"

"One of his sculptors. Romano purchased it for Rupert's housewarming gift."

"I could have choked!" Belinda whispered.

Allison collapsed, laughing.

"Mom's off again!" Nathaniel smiled at Stephen. Stephen-Paul Golding walked into the eruption of laughter from Allison. Wearing black contour jeans and an open neck black striped dress shirt, he handed over to Nathaniel a bottle of Sauvignon Blanc.

"It's good to see her laugh!" he commented, taking his seat opposite. While Allison waved to her friend, tears ran from her eyes.

Rupert was in the kitchen assisting his friend Marco. Marco was a chef at the *Monte De la Cristo*. When Rupert had found out that his mom was staying for dinner, he rang Marco to assist with the food. The restaurant prepared a five-course meal and Marco, and two waitresses transported the partly cooked food over to Santiago Del Porto.

Rachel had helped with the table layout of a Charles Montgomery dinner set and crystal wine glasses. Star-struck, she prepared herself for an exciting evening with Allison Templeton-Mancini.

"Alice, you have to stop!" Stephen said, chuckling.

A waitress from the restaurant interrupted the sniggering and served refreshments, while the food was being organised.

Belinda grabbed her drink from the young female and thanked her. The shoulder-length redhead spoke quietly towards Stephen. "Have you seen Alice's bodyguard? He's a hunk! Toy boy comes to mind."

Stephen leaned in. "What about Donny?"

"Oh, yeah. I love him, but I like to window shop! The height of him, I'll need a ladder!"

Allison again burst into hysterics.

Nathaniel walked in on the laughter. "Belinda, stop it!"

Rachel observed the scene, smiling. "She is so funny…"

"She is like it all the time! When Belinda and Mom are together, it is like an explosion." Nathaniel grinned. "Dad loves it."

The food was ready, and Nathaniel helped his giggling mother to the dining table. The soup starters sat in front of each guest. Belinda grunted as Rupert glared at her.

"Sorry Rup, it's tomato and grilled cheese, and I'm wearing a white dress!" Belinda moaned.

Rupert removed himself from the table and paced into the kitchen. Appearing with a tablecloth, he walked over to Belinda and tied it around her neck.

"Nice bib!" Nathaniel laughed.

Allison tried to restrain herself from laughing when she noticed a sapphire ring sitting on Rachel's wedding finger. Allison dropped her spoon.

"Have you got something to tell me, Rupert?" Allison said. "Rachel?"

Rupert smiled and placed his hand upon Rachel's free hand. "We are engaged!"

"You knew, you all knew!"

“Yes, I wanted to surprise you before you arrived in LA,” Rupert said.

Allison pushed her chair back and scurried around the table. Hugging the pair of them, she whispered, “You both have made me very happy tonight. Rachel welcome to the family.”

Rupert’s smile enlightened the entire dining room. “We are pregnant!”

Allison’s eyes bulged in shock. “I’m going to be a…when?”

Rachel replied, “October.

Belinda squealed in delight. “Congratulations. Champagne! Orange juice for Rachel!”

Allison sat back in her seat while Stephen laughed. “I thought this would make you happy,” he whispered.

“Wedding at Mancini Mansion, Rupert!” Allison announced, taking a sip of water to cool herself down.

“Yes, well, we would like it to be in April,” Rupert said.

Allison looked at Belinda; Belinda looked at Allison. “We need to plan ASAP!”

“Mother, please.” Nathaniel laughed. “Eat your soup first.”

****

Hotel Augustus - Milan - Italy

25th March 2006 - 1.00 p.m.

Fabian-Astor-Sylvester tugged at the red satin 1950s gown. Ella-Louisa Templeton-Mancini sighed.

"Darling, we are nearly ready!" Fabian exclaimed.

Ella-Louisa, nearly twenty-one, showed off her dynamic figure in a bodycon 1950s gown. Her raven hair curled to perfection, while her pale skin shone through her powdered features. Intense red lipstick created the perfect Eleanor Templeton-Jones.

The Scotch-clad designer leaned back, placed both hands on his hips, and nodded in approval. "Done!"

Two Sylvester assistants made haste and helped Ella-Louisa from the platform. Placing a red beret on her head, red gloves on her hands, and pointed suede slingback shoes on her feet.

The photographer, ready to shoot over a white backdrop, created the ideal lighting. Ella-Louisa posed as he shouted out instructions.

Fabian smiled at his triumph and whispered, "Perfection, beautiful."

"She is," a British voice intruded.

Fabian looked to his side. "Marquess of Harlsby."

"You should address me as my lord!" he laughed. "How the devil, are you, Fabian?"

"My darling Richard, I'm just perfect!" he said, patting the Marquess on his arm.

"Who is that? She is so beautiful!"

"You don't know who Ella-Louisa is? My God!" Fabian smirked. "Where have you been?"

Richard Tomkinson-Clifton was a twenty-nine-year-old, investment banker working in London.

"So, darling, what are you doing in Milan?" Fabian said, placing his hands into his tartan trouser pockets.

"Shopping!"

"London has the greatest shops."

"I was bored, so I flew out to Paris, then Milan, and next is New York!"

"On your own?" Fabian studied Ella-Louisa.

"With my sister!"

Fabian laughed. "Yes, I couldn't see you shopping on your own."

"How is Miles?"

"Busy, Montgomery. We have fashion week approaching upon us soon!"

"Penelope will want me to take her to New York's fashion week, I presume!" Richard scoffed. "Will this model be in your fashion week?"

Fabian turned to face him, his blue eyes intense, his designer stubble untouched. "My darling Richard, you haven't a clue who she is! She is not a full-time model. She is contracted to The House of Sylvester-Montgomery."

"My dear chap, that is very confusing for me." Richard shrugged.

Romano Mancini walked into the background. Wearing his typical black jeans and dress shirt in dark blue, he blended in well with the designer crew.

"My darling Romano! How good of you to join us." Fabian said, holding out both arms.

"Fabian, man. How is she doing?" Romano beamed his brilliant white smile.

"Excellent! Eleanor Templeton-Jones is reborn!" Fabian grinned.

Richard became quite dizzy. He was standing next to Romano Mancini, and that was his daughter whom Richard was drooling after.

"Who is this?" Romano smiled.

"The Marquess of Harlsby." Fabian replied.

"Oh. Do I bow to you, my lord?" Romano asked the dashing banker.

"No! I should bow to you, Mr Mancini," said the star-struck lord.

Fabian laughed. "Darlings. Romano, meet Richard. Richard, meet Romano."

Ella-Louisa had finalised her last shots of the day. Strolling over to her dad, she smiled. "I could murder a tea!"

"Baby, I will order you an Earl Grey!" Romano winked at her while she removed her pointed shoes.

"Earl Grey! You drink English tea?" Richard stepped in.

Ella-Louisa browsed up from her bent-down position and became overwhelmed. Romano held onto her. Standing above her was the most handsome man she had ever seen. Romano could see the connection between the two of them, so he intervened. "Yes, from an early age, we blame her mom!"

Richard placed his hand over his heart. "Allison Templeton-Mancini."

"Yep, my wife!" Romano grinned, still holding onto his daughter.

Ella-Louisa regained her balance and stood upright. Gazing at the gentleman, she blushed. Romano said, "We are staying in this hotel if you would like to join us for tea, my lord."

"My lord?" Ella-Louisa whispered.

"Yes, sorry. My name is Richard Tomkinson-Clifton, Marquess of Harlsby.

"You're a royal?" Ella-Louisa replied.

"As royal as I need to be. We do have to attend certain functions, but I am an investment banker in London." Richard explained, gazing into Ella's deep brown eyes.

"Right, Miss Mancini, go, and get changed. I will order tea in the lounge. Are you joining us, Richard?" Romano said.

"I would love to. Please, call me Dickie."

****

Hotel Augustus - Milan - Italy

25th March 2006 - 3.00 p.m.

Romano, sat comfortably in his armchair and ordered an Espresso along with two Earl Grey teas. Dickie remained tense sitting in his seat opposite.

"So, you like my daughter?" laughed Romano. "I can see the fascination, on both parts."

Richard spluttered.

"I know what it feels like. I was the same!" Romano tried to relax him.

Richard stared. "You do?"

"Yes, it happened to me. I met Alice in Germany when she was touring with Templeton. BAM! It hit me like a thunderbolt." Romano bashed his fist into his hand.

Richard jumped. "What happened?"

Romano lifted his left hand and displayed his gold band.

Richard was nervous as hell sitting across from the superstar and anticipated the arrival of his beautiful daughter.

"Look, I'm at a book signing later. Ella was supposed to join me, but if you would like dinner with her, I will give you my blessing," Romano leaned in. "There's only one thing…"

Richard gulped.

Romano pointed towards a huge cypress tree planted in a terracotta pot. "That guy sitting next to the tree is called Don, our bodyguard. He will keep watch.

"Watch what?" Richard said, sweating.

"I'm afraid people like us need protection. Don't get me wrong: they're all good guys, but it can be a pain. But less painful than getting shot."

"Am I gonna wake up with a dead animal in my bed?" he said.

Ella-Louisa arrived in style wearing an immense straw floppy hat. Richard stood up to greet Ella-Louisa who looked like a 1950s movie star.

Romano smiled. "You two look just like Theo and Eleanor."

"I've been dying for tea," Ella-Louisa said, taking her seat next to Richard.

“Nobody’s dying while security is in the room!” Romano said.

The hotel waitress transported two silver trays of teacups, saucers, milk, sugar, and a classic china teapot. Placing the trays on the designer table. Romano selected his espresso and nodded “*Grazie.*”

One of the waitresses smiled and replied, “*Ti serve qualcos’altro?*”

“*No, grazie*,” said Romano, holding his olive-skinned hand up towards the waitress.

Ella grinned at Richard. “He speaks great Italian!”

Richard laughed. “Romano Mancini is a great Italian.”

CHAPTER 7

Mancini Mansion - New Jersey

19th April 2006 - 9.00 a.m.

Velvet drapes hid the glorious morning sunlight. An abandoned mass of ruby fabric lay motionless upon the four-poster king-sized bed. Walking towards the clump of duvet, Romano Mancini carried a china cup and saucer of Earl Grey.

"You awake, baby?" he whispered.

An intense moan escaped from the depths of the bed coverings.

"Wakey, wakey," he whispered, putting the stylish cup down onto the bedside table. "I'll open the drapes and let some light into the room."

"No!" Allison screamed. "Ouch, my head!" she groaned, pulling herself up from her safety zone.

"You're not well, baby?" Romano fell onto his knees to observe his pale wife.

"My head is killing me. I just can't do light."

"Migraine? I'll call for aspirin," Romano said, standing up.

"Romano, I need a bowl," Allison mumbled, congested.

Romano grabbed the bedside burgundy telephone and rang for Simons. Allison remained seated upright, leaning against the pillows that Romano had assembled for her. Dark long curling hair crawled all over her white satin pyjamas.

A knock at the door: Romano ran across the room and grabbed a tray of aspirin and a bowl from Simons. Closing the door behind, he made haste towards the bed.

Allison grabbed the bowl and vomited into it. Romano recoiled at the smell descending from his wife.

Handing him the bowl, Allison flopped against the pillow. Romano opened the balcony doors and placed the bowl outside.

"Wow, that was something!" he said, pinching his nose.

"I need tissues." Allison sneezed.

Romano opened the packet of aspirin, went into the bathroom, and collected a glass of water. Sitting on the bed next to his wife, Romano handed over the aspirin, a box of tissues from the dresser, and water to Allison.

Swallowing two tablets, Allison drank a mouthful of water and passed the glass back to Romano. "I need sleep!"

"Baby, I'm bringing Maxi in." Romano said.

"No, I'll be ok." Allison grumbled.

"Three days until the wedding. Guests are arriving tomorrow," Romano pleaded. "I can't do this on my own!"

"Okay, bring him in," Allison sank under the duvet. "But leave the drapes closed."

Romano dispersed from the dark bedroom and scurried towards the grand staircase. Nathaniel and Angel Medley-Garrett walked arm in arm from his room.

“Morning!” Nathaniel smiled.

“Mr Mancini,” a soft English accent travelled over the airwaves towards Romano.

Romano looked around. “Morning, guys. Breakfast is in the conservatory this morning. Just got a lot on, you know, with the wedding!” Romano continued to pace towards his office.

Closing his door, Romano ran towards the black retro telephone. Picking up the handset, he dialled Maxi Spink.

“Hi,” a distant voice sounded at the end of the line.

“Maxi, it’s Romano. She’s not well.”

“What are Alice’s symptoms?” the faint voice asked.

“Vomiting, headache, light sensitivity, sneezing, and a blocked nose!” Romano panicked.

“Would be quicker to tell us what she doesn’t have,” Maxi shouted.

Romano placed the handset down and paced out into the foyer where Simons was watering a crystal vase of pink roses.

“Doctor Spink is on his way. Make sure no one sees him!” Romano said. “I don’t want to cause any distress.”

A voice called out. “Romano! Are you alright, my son?”

Romano looked up at the top of the staircase. "Just wedding planning, mama!"

Maria Mancini, seventy-nine, looked well for her age. Her grey up-do hair and pale make-up pronounced her beauty. Standing by her side was her husband, Giuseppe Mancini. The eighty-one-year-old resembled a sixty-year-old male. Romano prized olive oil for their youthfulness.

"You are always busy!" Maria laughed.

"Mama, Papa, breakfast is in the conservatory and Nat is in there!"

"My grandson!" Maria beamed.

The couple walked down the grand staircase holding hands. Romano grinned at the sight of his parents and wished that this would be Allison and himself at that age.

Maria kissed her son on the cheek and walked towards the conservatory with her husband. Romano hurried into the library and waited with anticipation for Doctor Spink to arrive. A sound from one of the burgundy Chesterfields erupted into a "Dad."

Romano turned around and found Sebastian reading.

"What are you doing in here?" Romano spoke.

"Reading," Sebastian laughed.

"Reading what, the breakfast menu?"

"I'm waiting for Sarah-Jane. She takes forever," Sebastian sighed.

"Grandmama Mancini is in the conservatory with Nat," Romano beamed, crossing his arms.

Sebastian put the book down on the coffee table and stood next to her father. Both wearing blue jeans and white shirts looked the image of one another. Apart from Sebastian towered over his father at six-foot-one. With similar hair styles, Sebastian's was raven black, and Romano, dark silver.

"Mom, is she in the conservatory?" Sebastian asked.

"Afraid not. Just taking a nap," Romano said, making excuses.

"Understandable. She is fifty!" Sebastian said, walking out of the library.

Romano shook his head. A black Porsche 911 Carrera pulled up outside the main entrance. A blonde-haired man stepped out, carrying a leather medical case. In seconds, Simons was on the scene guiding the doctor into the foyer.

Romano paced out of the library and checked the area for clearance and greeted Maxi. Pacing at speed up the grand staircase, both men disappeared into the dark master bedroom.

Allison, tangled within a comfortable lump of duvet and bedcovers, remained still. Maxi walked across to the four-poster bed and placed his medical bag on the floor

“Alice, it’s Maxi,” he said, while Romano lingered in the doorframe.

“Maxi?” she grunted.

“Romano tells me you’ve been ill.”

“Then I must be,” she mumbled again.

“Let me have a look at you,” Maxi removed his stethoscope from his bag.

Listening to her heart and examining her breathing, Maxi was happy with her performance.

Maxi pulled out a sample pot. “I need you to pee!”

“Can I help?” Romano cut in.

Maxi turned around and scowled at the silver-haired children’s author.

Allison walked over to the bathroom, barefoot, closing the door behind her.

“Pee?” Romano spat. “You’re sick.”

“I’m not sick, and neither is Alice.” Maxi’s thunderous look could have killed the author in one swoop. “Pregnant.”

“At fifty?”

“Yes.”

“A dad again?” Romano whispered.

Allison dragged her feet along the marble flooring, carrying her sample. Maxi retrieved the pot and removed a pregnancy test kit from his bag. Placing a drop of urine upon the tip, he anticipated two minutes of waiting, when he nodded. “You’re not pregnant!”

Allison breathed a sigh of relief whilst Romano seemed disappointment.

“I will need you in my clinic next week. I will prescribe you cyclizine for your sickness, steroid nasal spray, and sumatriptan for your migraine.” Maxi said, writing out the prescription. “I shall give this to Simons on my way out.”

“What do you think it is?” Allison mumbled.

“Hay fever!” Maxi answered. “You must take the required dose recommended.”

Romano snatched the sheet of paper from Maxi’s grip. “I will sort this!” he said, sprinting out of the bedroom and down the grand staircase.

“Alice, now Romano is not here, I’m going to be examining for menopause.”

“Is that what the sickness is?”

“Combined flushes and migraine. How are you feeling?” Maxi looked at Allison with observant eyes.

“Better, being sick made me feel better.”

“That’s the hay fever talking.” Maxi smiled.

Maxi left the room after his little chat with the superstar while Allison decided to walk back into the bathroom. Turning on the main light, Allison could deal with the bright intensity much better. Turning on the faucets of the luxury double free-standing bath, Allison poured in her favourite lavender bubbles. Leaving the water to cascade from the faucets, she strolled into the dark bedroom and attempted to open the drapes. With success both balcony doors allowed glorious sunshine to flow into the room.

Romano had sent Micky Connelly to collect Allison's prescription from the local drugstore. Romano paced up and down in the foyer, Rupert and Rachel bumped into him.

"Dad, what's wrong?" Rupert said, holding Rachel's hand.

"Waiting for a delivery," he grinned. "Your brothers and grandparents are having breakfast in the conservatory."

Rupert winked at his dad, and Rachel revealed her beautiful regal smile towards Romano.

The black Mercedes C-Class stopped outside the entrance. A muscular red-haired male strode towards the entrance doors, carrying a paper bag.

Romano opened the door and grabbed the bag from his grip.

"Thanks, Micky!" he said, running towards the staircase.

Barging into the bedroom, Romano noticed that the drapes had been opened and the smell of lavender hit the atmosphere. Rushing into the bathroom, he heard silence.

"Baby, are you, okay?" Romano fell on his knees beside the bath, still clutching the paper bag.

"I'm desperate for this bath, but I'm starved!" Allison sniffled.

"Right, I'll..."

"I'm going downstairs and I'm sitting with my family and a box of tissues," Allison demanded.

"Your usual?" Romano grinned at Miss Bossy coming back to life.

"Yes, please, but with extra portions!"

"Are you sure you're not pregnant?" Romano laughed.

"Me, pregnant?"

****

Mancini Mansion - New Jersey

22nd April 2006 - 11.30 a.m.

Staff rushed everywhere. Organising flowers, carrying trays and bottles of champagne outside the burgundy sitting room. Drinking Earl Grey, Allison Templeton-Mancini smiled at Kenneth Reen.

"Won't be long. She looks beautiful," Allison sighed.

"I never thought I would become so close to the Mancini family!" Kenneth answered, sitting in his navy-blue morning suit, gripping his china cup and saucer.

Allison laughed. "We are family and soon there will be an extra addition. I cannot wait!"

One hundred guests had made their way to their Chiavari seats, assembled in the immense gardens of Mancini Mansion.

A prodigious trapeze marquee displayed a cream and baby pink rose garland top table and ten round tables displaying pink and cream glass trumpet vases of roses. The ceiling was decorated in pink colourful drapes with an arrangement of cream roses. The marquee exhibited a fairy tale theme.

A bridesmaid giggled from behind Allison's view. Wearing a white sequin princess dress finished with a large satin pink bow, Fay-Elizabeth Pullman looked beautiful in her Sylvester-Montgomery designer dress. Wearing a baby pink rose head wreath and ballerina satin slippers, she portrayed beauty.

Allison removed herself from her seat and turned to witness the beautiful bridesmaid. A female wedding coordinator supervising Fay handed her a cream-and-pink rose posy.

"You look beautiful, Fay." Allison beamed.

Fay curtsied. "You look pretty too, Aunt Alice," remarked the blonde-haired girl.

Allison sported an exclusive Sylvester-Montgomery design: a huge pink-and-black brim hat placed at an immaculate angle over her up-do. Black belted jacket and a pink flowing scarf seated on her left shoulder. Completing the outfit, a pink-and-black-striped fishtail skirt.

Alexander Flora communicated by radio to the female coordinator standing in the foyer with Fay. Kenneth removed himself from the leather sofa and stepped towards the bottom of the grand staircase.

Fabian Astor-Sylvester and his team were arranging the final touches to Rachel's dress.

"My God!" he whispered, looking up at his stunning daughter.

Placing a deep, pink-nailed manicured hand on his right shoulder, Allison whispered, "She looks beautiful, Ken."

The baby pink off-the-shoulder lace-sleeved gown captured the fairy tale theme. Its sweeping train lay four feet behind Rachel.

Wearing a diamond tiara in her blonde updo and a cathedral vial in the coordinating colour, Rachel illuminated Mancini Mansion.

Kenneth kissed his daughter on her small dainty hand when she arrived at the bottom of the grand staircase. Allison kissed her cheek and tried to conceal her tears of happiness.

Posing happily for *Conception Magazine's* photographers, father and bride enjoyed the moment. Allison and Fabian also posed for the magazine.

Wearing his lavish red morning suit, Fabian said to Rachel, "You look stunning, darling!"

The wedding coordinators soon ushered Allison forward along with Fay at the front of the double doors. Cameras continued to click and flash while the two of them positioned themselves onto the red carpet. The bride and her father followed.

Allison witnessed all the guests facing forward. Her sons Rupert and Nathaniel waited, dressed in their navy-blue morning suits, against a crystal arch.

"Oh, my boys!" she whispered as the sun rays twinkled against the clear cuts of crystal.

The orchestra commenced playing *Salut d'Amour* while the wedding coordinators counted in time to the violin tones.

Allison smiled at the wedding guests as she stepped in time and noticed Jake and Helen Pullman waving at their daughter.

Fay and Allison strode left and waited for Kenneth and Rachel to take their places. Finally, Rachel stood beside Rupert, still facing forward while she passed her bouquet to Allison.

The minister placed Rachel's hand upon Rupert's and announced, "Who gives this woman to be married to this man?"

Kenneth replied, "I do."

****

Mancini Mansion - New Jersey

22nd April 2006 - 3.00 p.m.

Crystal glasses radiated against sparkling champagne bubbles. Golden swirled crockery clattered against assorted conversions. An overspill of pink garland roses trailed elegantly against jacquard white table wear.

Nathanial Templeton-Mancini clinked a champagne glass with his knife. Viewing the celebrity guests seated at round tables, he commenced with his speech.

"Welcome to the wedding of Rupert and Rachel Templeton-Mancini. Today promises to become permanent and friends become family. Thank you for joining us on such a wonderful occasion. Let's raise our glasses to Rupert and Rachel."

Romano glanced at Allison sitting next to Rupert. Leaning in, Romano whispered, "Thank heavens he didn't screw up!"

Allison laughed and toasted her loving son and his bride. The bride and groom kissed. Nathaniel remained standing in his blue morning suit, sipping champagne. He walked towards table five, smiling at Angel Medley-Garrett. Placing himself in front of her, he knelt on one knee.

Romano's dark brown eyes bulged. "I knew he would screw this up!"

"Dad, I gave him permission," Rupert whispered.

The elegant marquee fell into silence and paused for Nathaniel's proposal. Oliver Dupont pulled out his mobile and rang his people. "Nat Mancini is going to propose. Cameras, now!"

"Oliver, darling, do you have to work today?" scoffed Sebastian, lounging against the table.

Belinda and Donny Davis cut in. "Oliver, this is breaking news!"

Oliver beamed. "I've got it covered," he winked at Sebastian.

Allison placed her soft, manicured hand over her mouth while Charles Medley-Garratt applauded the superstar.

Gazing into Angel's green eyes, he said, "I can't imagine growing old with anyone else, nor do I want to. I know you're the only one I want to share the rest of my life with. Marry me."

Angel beamed with happiness. "Yes, Nat I will marry you."

The marquee exploded into boisterous celebrations. Nathaniel pulled himself up and drew Angel into his arms. He kissed his fiancée like a medieval king kissed his queen.

Romano stood to applaud his son. "Didn't think he had it in him."

Allison remained seated, dabbing her eyes with a tissue. Tugging at Romano's morning jacket. "Romano, he doesn't have a ring!"

"Figures," Romano sighed, placing both hands on his hips.

Allison yanked off a small opal ring from her right hand. "Romano, take this over to him. It's his grandmama's."

Romano accepted the ring from Allison and paced over to the happy couple. "Nat," Romano whispered, placing the ring into Nathaniel's huge hand.

Nathaniel glanced down at his hand and quickly smiled. "Angel, I thought we could choose your ring together. But today, would you wear my grandmama's ring?"

Angel accepted with a huge nod and grin and the vintage opal and diamond ring slid tightly onto her wedding finger. "It just fits," she whispered, gazing at the sparkling gemstone.

"We'll have to return it!" He leaned in and kissed her.

The bride and groom toasted the happy couple while Allison walked over and kissed the pair of them, welcoming Angel to the family.

Celebrations continued and the beautiful nine-tier fondant wedding cake prepared itself for slicing. *Conception Magazine* got the exclusive new shots of the married couple cutting into the cake and the newly engaged couple feeding cake to each other.

Sebastian, Ella-Louisa, and Benedict laughed, observing the photo shoot. “Next they’ll be having a foursome!”

Dickie and Penelope Tomkinson-Clifton smirked. “Are they always together?”

“Rup lives next door to Nat. He’s Nat’s director!” Ella-Louisa said.

Marina Mancini hugged her son. “Another wedding soon!” She beamed in delight.

“Yes, mama, another wedding!” Romano sighed.

****

Mancini Mansion - New Jersey

23rd April 2006 - 2.00am.

Ella-Louisa stood with her hands on her hips, observing herself in a French dress mirror, she whispered, “Right, I’m going to do this.”

Opening the door, Ella looked up and down the passageway for clearance. Closing her bedroom door behind her, she made a quick getaway towards Dickie’s room.

The mansion was silent apart from the staff downstairs cleaning up after Rupert’s extravagant wedding. Tiptoeing through the shadows of the passageway, Ella stopped at a solid walnut door. Tapping against the wood grain, she could hear snoring bellowing from the other side. Gripping the brass door handle, Ella opened the unlocked door.

Stepping inside the Regency-style room, darkness invaded every available space and Ella struggled to see clearly. A body lay under the gold-coloured duvet, creating a mountain summit on the king-sized bed. Ella locked the door behind her and crept around the bed. Undressing down to her underwear and stockings, she hoisted up the duvet cover and slid underneath.

A deep, tantalising moan sounded from underneath the covers. Ella-Louisa cuddled up against a naked body. Feeling his bare legs upon hers sent shivers down her spine.

"What are you doing in here, Miss Ella?" a deep, groggy voice sounded.

Whispering back, she replied, "I need to be with you, Dickie."

"Oh, Ella, you really sneaked into my bed?" he groaned, pulling her towards him.

"It's time."

Dickie placed his warm full-bodied lips upon hers. "Are you sure?"

Nodding, she deeply kissed him back, moaning. She felt his strong, muscular body rolling above her while he removed her bra. Groaning into her breasts, Dickie removed her pink panties.

"You're a virgin!"

"Not tonight," she moaned.

****

Castrum Place - Rye - New York

25th April 2006 - 2.00 p.m.

A calamitous infatuation fermented within the household of Castrum Place. After cremating his beloved wife Miranda on the 21st of September 2005, Paul Freidman had gone demented. Placing his wife's ashes under a shrine of photographs of Helen Pullman.

Candles flickered inside a darken room where only he himself was permitted to enter. The solitary room was painted dark blue, but the heavy drapes remained closed. On one side of the wall displayed every newspaper cutting of Helen, while the other side displayed actual photographs of her with blonde and dark hair.

In the centre of the room positioned a dark blue fireside armchair. Paul would sit for hours staring at the photographs.

There was evidence of insanity, each photograph was measured accurately with the same distance between the next photographs.

Paul Freidman had hired a private investigator to monitor Helen's movements. He paid him well.

Sitting in his spacious modern office, Paul Freidman leaned back against his cream leather desk chair. Gripping a glass of whiskey, he grinned at two suited males sitting in front of him.

"Surveillance?" Sandy Hill announced.

"Who the hell told you we are under surveillance?" Paul scowled at his logistics executive.

"We got glows everywhere," he muttered back in his deep vibrating voice.

"The Western European warehouses have to close, Paul!" Miles Peterson cut in.

Paul slammed his fist down hard on his brushed glazed oak desk.

Miles leaned in. "You'll go down if you keep them running."

"Computers, they're using computers," Paul said. "Who are they to scan my stock?"

"Logistics. Booking consignments in and out of their loading docks."

"I'll buy the docks myself!" Paul snarled.

"And give them even more evidence?" Miles said, staring at Sandy.

"Why own a shipping company if we can't ship?"

"You can't just purchase every port in Europe!" Miles answered back.

A knock at the door stopped the conversation. "Come in!" Paul yelled.

Two bruisers in grey suits walked into the office, cracking their knuckles.

Paul stood up. "This meeting is over!"

Miles and Sandy walked out of Castrum Place. Standing on the gravel driveway Miles pulled out his mobile phone and dialled a familiar number.

"Jonathan, start closing Europe! The money transfers are complete."

Miles hung up and walked over to his Porsche, high fiving Sandy. Sitting behind his sports steering wheel Miles looked at Castrum Place for the very last time.

"Goodbye…" He whispered, has he sped off down the shadowy lane.

CHAPTER 8

Arc Hopes Hospital - New Jersey

28th April 2006 - 10.30 a.m.

Allison read her phone messages while the silver limousine manoeuvred into its reserved parking lot at the rear of the private hospital. Tomas Meier, Allison's handsome bodyguard, opened the rear passenger door.

"Miss Alice," spoke a deep sensual voice.

Allison looked up. "Okay, I'm ready."

Tomas escorted the brunette superstar into the rear entrance to avoid any publicity. A middle-aged nurse greeted Allison and Tomas and accompanied the couple towards Maxi's office.

"Alice, please step into my abode. Tomas, you wait outside," Maxi said. "Women and children first."

Tomas nodded and immersed himself into a lime green bucket chair, grabbing the latest edition of *Conception Magazine.*

Maxi closed the door behind while Allison positioned herself onto a mustard sofa.

"Cool couch, Maxi," she said, removing her Sylvester-Montgomery sunglasses.

"Renovation. It's the latest colour," Maxi said. "Apparently."

"How exciting."

"Any hot flashes?"

"Yes…"

"Night sweats?"

"Yes."

"Uh, dryness?"

"Yes…."

"Difficulty sleeping?"

"No…"

"Confusion?"

"Yes…"

"Mood swings?"

"What do you think I am, a nutjob!"

Maxi checked the box and stared into the light reflecting onto his round rim spectacles. "I believe you are going through menopause."

"Me? Menopause?" Allison muttered.

"I'm going to run some tests and suggest hormone replacement therapy."

"Can I still have sex?" Allison said. "If not, Romano will put me up for adoption!"

Maxi laughed. "There's always lubrication.

"Always?" she said. "Remind me not to come has a woman next time."

****

Pullman House - Pennsylvania

29th April 2006 - 1.00 p.m.

A warm southern breeze danced amongst the white oak trees, scattered against the moss green hills of Pullman house. The sun smiled kindly upon the viridescent landscape while candy floss clouds gently advanced eastwards.

Fay-Elizabeth Pullman played with her handheld gaming console while sitting on her cushioned window seat. Staring through the large arch window, she noticed a black truck parked outside the secured double gates.

“Mummy! Mummy!” she shouted.

“Fay, darling, don’t shout,” Helen said, standing in the chequered foyer.

“There is a car parked at the gate!” Fay replied, sitting on the top step.

Helen called Win Millett, her thirty-five-year-old bodyguard. Win appeared from behind. “Mrs Pullman…”

“Fay saw a suspicious vehicle parked outside the gates.”

“I will check the security camera.” Win walked off towards the camera room where another two guards were on duty.

“Mummy, it’s not good.” Fay said. “Is it?”

“People lose their way from time to time and must park their vehicles. Map reading!” Helen grinned.

Still remaining seated on the top step, she said, "When is Daddy coming home?"

Helen looked at her daughter. "Next week. He is in Washington on business."

"Can I have a glass of lemonade?"

The grey-haired mother of one laughed. "Of course, sweetie."

Fay ran down the staircase in her white woollen tights and red dungaree dress.

"Where are your shoes?" Helen looked down at her bare feet.

"Upstairs," she grinned.

Lifting her daughter up into her arms "Don't worry, we shall drink our lemonade shoeless!"

Walking into the sitting room, Fay took her place on the large leather sofa while a Pullman housemaid carried in a tray of two refreshing glasses of lemonade.

Win approached Helen and the two of them slipped out of the sitting room into the hallway.

"We are on lockdown!" Win whispered.

"The truck?"

"Plates don't match any database in the country."

"My God!" Helen said.

****

Pullman House - 9.00 p.m.

Fay had retired to bed while a huge gentle giant of a guy in a black suit positioned himself outside her bedroom. Automatic shutters were activated, securing the windows in Pullman House.

Helen had explained earlier to the Pullman staff that they must remain silent about the lockdown because of Fay. Taking a glass of warm milk to bed, Helen said goodnight to another new bodyguard sitting outside her room. Closing her door, she strolled over to the king-sized bed and placed her warm drink down on a side table. Picking up the handset of her mobile, she dialed Jake.

A familiar voice sprang to life from the other end. "Darling, are you okay?" Jake said.

"Yes, so is Fay," she sighed.

"Sorry I had to order a lockdown, but I can't risk losing you."

"Freidman?"

"I can't go into it," Jake replied.

"Should I ask the guards?"

"Big guys. They make us look small!" Jake laughed to ease the tension.

"School next week for Fay. Work for me at Dayton's."

"I can't let you go to the office. Can you work from home?" Jake said.

"That bad?"

"Well…"

"What about school?"

"Look, Helen, I will sort school, we are under a lockdown, and it breaks my heart that I am not with you. Next year I'm resigning from my position in politics. I'm…"

"I'm what?" Helen gasped.

"I'm going to be a partner in my own law firm. It's all arranged, Pennsylvania!"

"You're going back into law?" Helen whispered, staring at the soft yellow shadows cast from her luxury bedside lamp.

"W & J Pullman Law."

"The offices?" Helen jumped in.

"Philadelphia. Where else?"

"Home!" screeched Helen, relieved.

Jake laughed. "I need family. My time in Washington is over!"

"How long have you been organising this move?"

"Twelve months. I purchased the offices in January, hired structural designers," Jake laughed.

"You have been busy, Mr Pullman," Helen laughed back.

"I did this move for you, like I did Washington for my pops. We will get through this with Freidman, even if it's the last thing I do!" Jake scowled.

****

Castrum Place - Rye - New York

29th April 2006 - 10.00 p.m.

Paul Freidman lounged on his dark blue fabric fireside chair, staring at his shrine of photographs. Groaning, he reached out his hand towards a side table and pulled out a tissue from an unused box. A bang at the door startled him. "What?" he yelled, tugging up his grey boxers.

"Sir, two gentlemen to see you," called out the butler.

"Yeah, yeah! I'll be right out," he said, pulling his trousers up.

Fastening his belt, he adjusted himself and strolled from the room, locking the door behind him.

"Paul, there is no way we can get into Pullman's House," said a suited bald man standing in the hallway.

"My office, now!" Freidman said.

The other intruder was smaller than his colleague and followed Paul into the spacious modern office.

"We kept tabs on her. She has a bodyguard."

"Bastard!" Paul slammed his fist down onto his desk. "I don't care if you need to kill everyone in that school zone! I want her!"

"Speak up, Paul, the police couldn't hear you."

Paul glared. "The feds may have wired up our warehouses, but they would never expect me to bring her here." Paul walked around his white maple office. "I want her here! Understand! Now get out!"

Quickly leaving the office, the two smartly dressed men walked out of the entrance of Castrum Place. Sudden footsteps sounded on the uneven gravel. Grabbing the smallest thug from behind, a muscular arm pulled him around his neck into the dense heavy foliage.

The bald thug urgently looked around when another shadow dragged him into the foliage as well. The sound of running feet hit the gravel and stopped by a parked truck. Headlights illuminated the driveway has the truck hit reverse. The back doors opened, and two lifeless bodies were thrown into the back. The screeching of tyres hit the dusty track and the truck was gone.

****

Rye - New York - 5th May 2006

Birds chirped as the warm spring breeze rustled against the bright green leaves. A middle-aged male walked on a dry path with his black Labrador Max. Holding a stick, he swung with all his might and released the stick towards his dog. Missing his dog, the stick hurdled over the animal and down an embankment. The Labrador bounced towards its target and disappeared.

The man ran after his dog and stopped by a stream of water flowing between the embarkment of rocks and tree roots. He spotted Max searching for his stick when two naked bodies with their throats cut floated face-down in the gushing water.

Shaking and panicking, the dog walker pulled out his mobile phone and rang 911. Trying to get his dog to heel, the man ran into a clearing and vomited. Within ten minutes the sound of sirens echoed through the woods.

Two traffic patrol cars manoeuvred down the uneven track, while a black truck and two unmarked cars followed. The dog walker waved at the oncoming vehicles to stop.

Five vehicles parked next to one another and two suited males from the last unmarked vehicle climbed out. Walking towards the shocked dog walker, four uniformed officers followed the detectives.

"Mr Kane, my name is Detective Monroe, and this is my colleague, Detective Lee. You have found two bodies, is that correct?" said Monroe, brandishing his badge.

The dog walker pointed towards the embankment and nodded. Detective Lee patted Max on the head and pulled out a worn notebook from his suit jacket.

Four uniformed officers sealed the crime scene with caution tape, while a forensic photographer made his way down the embankment. Another truck pulled up and two more white coverall men entered the sealed location.

"We need a statement, and your dog don't speak much English," Detective Monroe said. The cop guided Mr Kane over towards the first marked patrol car. Opening the back passenger door, he and Max were placed inside the vehicle.

"Looks like a gang killing!" A voice sprang up from behind Monroe.

Joe Monroe turned around and another suited detective grinned. "A 'gang killing,' Jack? They teach you that in college?"

"Ten years ago, I was on a case just like this. We believe these murders are linked," the American Caribbean detective said.

"What's the theory?" Monroe replied, looking around the area.

"A guy called Paul Freidman!"

"The millionaire?" Monroe looked puzzled. "Why him?"

"We think he killed Eva Moulin, Stella Freidman and four crew members of the Proclivity 2. I have been on his case for years." Jack sighed.

"And these two boys?" Joe pointed towards the embankment.

“Probably his thugs. No good to him dead.”

“Don’t swim so good, either” Monroe whispered.

“Every time Freidman takes a leak, three feds start snapping crime scene photos!”

“He’s crooked?” Monroe gripped the trunk of the marked patrol car.

“You’re not from around here, huh?” Jack asked. “Everybody is crooked who deals with Freidman.”

More people arrived at the scene and Mr Kane the dog walker gave his statement and was driven home with Max. Detective Monroe and Detective Lee made their way back to the station – first job, witnesses.

The two naked bodies were bagged and driven to the local morgue for a post-mortem examination. Detective Jack Henry leaned against a tree trunk and lit his cigar, while observing the chaos that Freidman had caused once again.

He said inhaling the sweet raptures of nicotine. “Time is running out, Freidman!”

CHAPTER 9

Liberty House Hotel - Central London

1st July 2006 - 11.30 a.m.

Jono Murrey and Don Spelling sipped ground roasted coffee in the enchanting Victoria Suite. The six-foot-two bodyguards styled themselves with tailored black suits and designer haircuts. Concealing themselves behind green foliage, the bodyguards laughed in conversation while two males chattered with their partners over a selection of tea and coffee.

Nathaniel Templeton-Mancini held his fiancée's soft, white hand while she chatted with his sister Ella-Louisa.

Nathaniel had proposed to Angel Medley-Garrett on the afternoon of his brother's wedding reception. Due to his filming schedule, the lovers couldn't see one another for weeks and Nathaniel had decided to arrange a full shopping weekend in London to purchase a ring for Angel at the first available opportunity.

Ella-Louisa insisted on accompanying her brother so she could spend time with Dickie the Marquess of Harlsby.

The last time they had seen one another was at Rupert's wedding on the 22nd of April 2006.

Flying into London airport on the extravagant Mancini 757 was thrilling: no press, no TV coverage, it was heaven.

Both siblings couldn't contain themselves. Exhilaration erupted within the transatlantic flight.

Both resided at Liberty House Hotel in central London. The balcony views of Tower Bridge and the Tower of London animated the siblings.

Nathaniel and Angel accommodated The Peach Apricot Penthouse Suite, while Ella-Louisa occupied The Rose Apple Penthouse Suite. Ella-Louisa loved the sophisticated design of mixed pinks and apple green, The Victorian brushed gold metal bed in the master bedroom completed Ella's expectations.

Nathaniel wasn't fussed either way as long as he could make love to Angel every night. In Nathaniel's words, "What did it matter what colour the rooms were?"

Nathaniel and Angel had arranged an appointment at 12:30 p.m. in Oxford Street - Jewels of London. The exquisite shop was exclusive to the prestige by appointment only.

Nathaniel thought he could just walk into the jewellers and purchase a ring. The management explained by intercom the procedure, and an appointment was arranged for the next day.

Ella-Louisa had made plans to visit Dickie's stately home in Harlsby, one hour and twenty minutes away from

London. Don Spelling walked over to the giggling couple drinking Earl Grey tea. "Your car is ready, Miss Ella."

Ella-Louisa stretched her neck, looking up at the imposing bodyguard. "Ready, Don."

Dickie Tomkinson-Clifton grabbed Ella-Louisa's hand and pulled her from her seat. Ella wore a long vintage 1950s navy blue swing dress and slingbacks. Her long, curling raven black hair contributed to her style.

"See you guys at seven," Ella said.

Nathaniel cuddled his sister goodbye. Ella, Dickie, and Don disappeared from the delightful Victoria Suite.

"Another drink?" Nathaniel asked his fiancée.

"No, Nat. If we keep this up, I'll need an intervention."

"You need to relax." He raised his black eyebrows.

"We have my ring to sort. I want this to be right!"

"We'll discuss in bed… all afternoon!"

"Nathaniel Templeton-Mancini!"

"So, you do know my name."

****

Jewels Of London - London

1st July 2006 - 12.45 p.m.

"Mr Mancini, Jewels of London contribute to a unique collection of South African diamonds," the jeweller announced, placing a tray of expensive diamonds on the table.

"It's Templeton-Mancini," Nathaniel replied.

Sitting in an exclusive private room of red velvet high back chairs and a sterling silver table, Nathaniel brushed his fingers through his sweeping hair.

Angel knew Nathaniel was stressed because she had seen him on numerous of occasions repeating this action. "We would like to see the emeralds, please," Angel cut in.

Nathaniel glanced at her. "Will your eyes match the emeralds, or the emeralds match your eyes?"

Angel giggled while the jeweller exchanged trays, placing the emerald collection in front of Angel's view.

She gasped. "Oh, I love these."

Nathaniel lifted his head up in response from his fiancée.

"Can I try this one, please?" she asked the jeweller.

The jeweller wearing white gloves removed the ring from the tray. Holding the green, emerald diamond ring, he placed it onto Angel's third finger.

Nathaniel peered closely at the ring.

"Oh, it's so beautiful." She glanced lovingly at the ring, holding her hand into the light.

Nathaniel jumped in "How much?"

The jeweller stared at Nathaniel and wrote the figure on a piece of paper.

Nathaniel grabbed the paper and spoke "£20,428.25, not a problem."

Angel couldn't breathe.

"We'll take it!" Nathaniel handed the note back to the jeweller.

"The ring is available, but we have to ensure that the fitting is correct."

"Do your thing!" Nathaniel said.

A female assistant walked into the room and greeted Angel, measuring her manicured finger with a metal gauge sizing tool. The ring could be delivered to the hotel later that day.

Nathaniel paid for the ring outright with his platinum credit card, while the administrator entered his details into their system. The female administrator wheezed, "You are the film star! Nathaniel Templeton-Mancini!"

"With a hyphen," he said.

The female administrator excused herself and dispersed from the office to have words with the jeweller while Angel persisted in the next room with the ring estimator.

A loud cough interrupted the silence. The jeweller strolled into the admin office and bowed. "Please join us with your fiancée in the next room."

Nathaniel placed his credit card back into his Sylvester-Montgomery wallet and joined them. He laughed when he witnessed his fiancée enjoying a sparkling glass of champagne.

"I'd like to apologise for my rudeness," the jeweller said.

Nathaniel looked at the well-dressed man and commented, "We are all the same. It doesn't matter whether I am a film star or a porn star," Nathaniel grabbed his glass of champagne. "Cheers!"

****

Harlsby-Hall - Harlsby - 1st July 2006 - 1.30 p.m.

Ella-Louisa and Dickie Tomkinson-Clifton gazed at one another through the glorious garden sunshine.

"It's so beautiful and peaceful here!" she whispered into the succulent breeze.

"This is my home, apart from the penthouse in London," he responded. Wearing denim jeans and a short sleeved pale blue shirt, Dickie felt relaxed.

Ella-Louisa pointed towards a church in the grounds. "What is that building?"

Dickie smiled "Family chapel for christenings, weddings, and funerals."

She stopped and looked at him. "A cemetery!"

"All the Tomkinson-Cliftons are buried here, apart from Elizabeth."

“Yes, she is buried with her husband in Pennsylvania.”

“Jake’s mother…very sad.”

“The Templeton-Millers are buried in Switzerland,” she sighed, thinking about her grandparents.

“Don’t you belong to the Templetons? Viscount Templeton?”

Ella-Louisa replied, “Yes my great-grandmama was Viscountess Templeton and my second cousin is Viscount Templeton.”

“That’s a story you should tell me one day.” Dickie smiled.

Turning around to view the twenty-bedroom mansion in all its glory, Ella-Louisa could see the love stories of the Bronte Sisters. The setting was perfect: the Victorian structure, fountained gardens, and miles of countryside.

She turned towards Dickie. “I don’t want to go home!”

Dickie opened his blue eyes and gazed into Ella-Louisa’s. “What are you saying, Ella?”

“I’m totally and utterly in love with you,” she said.

Dickie smiled “My God, I didn’t know how to tell you. I fell in love with you in Milan.”

“You did?” Ella stared.

Dickie got down on one knee and pulled out a ring box from his jeans pocket. Opening the delicate green velvet box, he produced the most beautiful ring Ella-Louisa had ever seen.

"Ella-Louisa Templeton-Mancini, will you marry me?" He gazed into her deep brown eyes.

"Yes, yes, yes!" she squealed, jumping up and down.

Dickie stood up and placed the diamond ruby ring onto her third finger left hand. "My mother's engagement ring."

Ella sighed. "I love it."

Dickie held Ella in his arms, aiming his tender lips against hers. Softly, delicately with inhaling breaths, the warmth of her skin against his. The lovers embraced for more than fifteen minutes.

"Live with me here at Harlsby! Tonight! Forever!"

****

Liberty House Hotel - Central London-

1st July 2006 - 7.00 p.m.

Champagne sparkled in crystal flutes. Clinking of crockery resonated against laughter and individual conversations in the Albert Suite dining room.

Nathaniel Templeton-Mancini, dressed to perfection in his Sylvester dark grey suit and silver tie, held his fiancée's hand, rubbing his large, masculine fingers over the huge emerald stone placed on her wedding finger. Angel flourished with happiness and smiled at him. "They should be here soon!" Her soft English accent sounded against the busy atmosphere.

"Ella is always late," said Nathaniel.

Within moments, a 1920s style darked haired woman and her handsome man walked up to the gold-crested table.

"Sorry we're late. We had one hell of a day!" Ella-Louisa said, taking her place next to Dickie.

"Beautiful day," beamed Angel, holding out her emerald ring finger.

"That is so beautiful!" squealed Ella, grabbing Angel's hand and looking close at the stone.

"I am so pleased for you both. I could never wish for a better sister-in-law!"

The 1920s evening dress became the theme of conversation. Angel, wearing a designer black evening dress, said, "Wow, you look like a movie star all the time."

"I'm a model, not a movie star. Movie stars have talent!" Ella explained, pointing a finger in jest.

Angel looked across at her, finger waggling. "Oh my God! You're engaged!"

"We are!" laughed Ella.

"This afternoon in my gardens," Dickie smiled, grabbing Ella-Louisa's hand.

"Congratulations." Angel hugged Ella-Louisa.

Nathaniel looked shocked. “You too?”

“I have been carrying the ring around with me…since I don’t know when, waiting for that special moment...!” Dickie laughed.

“Oh, Nat…. there is a family chapel in the grounds of the Hall. We are marrying there! Also, I move into Harlsby-Hall tomorrow…I’m not flying home!” Ella announced.

Dickie held Ella’s hand even tighter. “My future wife will be accustomed to a Harlsby way of living.”

Ella-Louisa blushed.

Angel didn’t understand Dickie’s theory and watched her fiancé in deep thought.

“What? Mom and Dad are going to be upset. Just a minute, you said Dickie’s got a chapel?”

“Yes,” Ella replied before ordering her drink.

“Can we marry there as well?” Nathaniel barked.

“A double wedding?” Dickie cut in.

“Yeah,” Nathaniel said while he was ordering a glass of red.

“I can’t see that being a problem.” Dickie looked at Ella. “Only if my future wife agrees!”

Ella-Louisa jumped in. “That will be so cool. What do you think, Angel?”

“I love it. When?”

“Next month, twenty-eight days from when we give notice,” Dickie said.

“English rules are stupid! I can get married tomorrow in Vegas!” scoffed Nathaniel.

“You will become a Lady,” Angel interrupted.

“I’d like to think I’m already a lady.”

“Ella will become The Marchioness of Harlsby,” Dickie cut in.

“Does that mean I will have to bow to my sister?” Nathaniel remarked.

****

Aquifolium Mansion - New Jersey - 3rd July 2006

Allison drove her red Factory Works Mini, accompanied by her bodyguard Tomas.

“The emerald mosaic drive looks like something out of Oz!” Tomas said.

“Just wait until you see the house!”

As the Mini turned the corner, a stone-turreted mansion with arched windows and rustic oak doors came into view.

“Good God!” Tomas whispered.

“Camelot!” Allison laughed.

Parking outside the spectacular home of Sebastian and Oliver Dupont, Allison jumped out of the driver’s side door while Tomas struggled to move his legs from his cramped position.

The Dupont staff removed Tomas from the sports Mini while a familiar voice sounded, “Darling!” Sebastian held out his arms and strolled towards Allison.

“Sebastian!” Allison called across, wearing black capri three quarter length pants and a tied chequered shirt.

“You look like a 1950s actress,” smiled Sebastian, hugging his favourite girl.

“Ella’s choice!” she smiled.

“How is my little girl?”

“She is growing up!” Allison peeped at Sebastian through her cat eye sunglasses. “I have news!”

Sebastian clapped. “Come into my parlour and we shall have tea!”

The two friends went into Sebastian’s foyer. Solid dark oak flooring and sheer white walls created peace and tranquility. Huge delineations of black and white castle etchings were assembled onto the exquisite wallcoverings.

The grand staircase climaxed in solid oak and black carpeted steps. A glass wrought iron 24-armed chandelier sparkled its black and silver gems.

Tomas opened his eyes wide at the scene. Walking into Sebastian’s sitting room, Allison placed herself onto a black and red baroque six-seater sofa. While Sebastian sat comfortably in his large black dragon throne chair, Tomas sat on another sofa opposite Sebastian.

Observing the sitting room, Tomas noticed another black dragon throne chair that coordinated with Sebastian's. The dark oak coffee table displayed white marbled coasters. No drapes, only automatic tints completing the look at the enormous windows.

Sebastian's point of view was that at the age of sixty-five, it was time to move into the twenty-first century, so he used the influences of King Arthur.

The Dupont staff carried silver trays of Earl Grey tea into the sitting room. Wearing black dress trousers, a white dress shirt, pink neckerchief, and black leather clogs, Sebastian surpassed his modern look.

"Please tell me about Ella?" Sebastian smiled, selecting the teapot, and pouring tea into the coordinating china cups.

Allison asked Tomas if he would like tea, but he declined. "You know the English lord who accompanied her to Rupert's wedding?"

"Very handsome," Sebastian said.

"I think they will marry!" she continued, while selecting her steaming black tea.

"How do you know?"

"Maternal instincts. She is with him now in England. Nathaniel is there with Angel."

"Oh, yes, the ring!" Sebastian nodded.

"Engaged on Rupert's day, but couldn't be together until now," Allison sighed. "Ring shopping trip."

"Yes, I do believe we have all encountered time apart," Sebastian sipped his tea.

"You can say that again!" Allison scoffed.

"How are the schools coming along?"

"We have three schools built so far. My plan is to visit Africa next year, taking your husband with me."

"Oliver will love that! *Conception Magazine* will love that!" he grinned.

"You are coming along as well. I can't have one Dupont without the other!"

Sebastian's face lit the white glowing room into all its glory.

"I have a feeling, Sebastian, that Ella will not be coming home," Allison stated.

"Why?" he said, surprised.

"She is settled in England. Mama always wanted to return to England, and Switzerland was her substitute. Ella-Louisa is Eleanor Templeton-Jones."

A roaring sound vibrated outside Sebastian's stylish house. A Silver Jaguar XK parked behind Allison's red Mini.

A knock at the double oak doors interrupted the conversation. Romano paced into the elegant sitting room "Alice," he puffed.

"Romano, my dear man, please sit!" Sebastian stood up from his chair.

Romano looked at the enormous carved oak fireplace. "That is so cool!"

Sebastian turned towards the magnificent centre piece of his room and noticed the sword and shield above it. "Hot, Romano. It's a fireplace," he smirked.

"Are those real swords?" Romano pulled up his nose, not sure what to make of any of it.

"That Excalibur cost me a quite a packet, let me tell you."

"Coffee?" Sebastian interrupted.

"Black," Romano said, taking his place next to Tomas.

"What's so urgent you need black?" Allison sighed.

"Ella-Louisa." Romano spoke.

Allison shrugged. "What about her?"

"She's engaged!"

"Excellent!"

"Excellent! She's only twenty!" he bellowed.

"Twenty-one in December!" smiled Allison, winding her husband up.

Sebastian stepped in. "Calm down, Romano! We understand that Ella-Louisa is engaged to that beautiful English lord…."

"She is living with him, and they are getting married on the 5th of August. At the lord's castle!" Romano spluttered.

"I always loved King Arthur and Merlin." Allison smiled.

"This is not amusing, Alice." Romano brushed both hands through his hair.

"I'll have to inform Fabien."

"Ella's already notified him; his team are flying out next week."

Allison clapped. "Oh, goodie. I can have a new outfit. Is purple royal enough?"

"Are you listening to me?" Romano glared at his wife trying to drink the remaining residue of her tea.

Banging her teacup down "Look! She is in love!" she shouted and then stopped herself.

"Okay, okay." Romano held both hands up in surrender. "No need to shout."

Composing herself again "Right! Our daughter is getting married. Let's enjoy it!"

Romano looked. "That's not all. Nathaniel…"

"What has he done?" she sighed.

"It's a double wedding!" Romano grunted.

"In England?"

"Where else?"

"Marvellous. Two children married at once. All over in one day!" Allison smiled.

Sebastian laughed. "Excellent! Oliver will be able to inform the London office for *Conception* and I will invest in a new morning suit from Sylvester-Montgomery. You are right, Alice, purple!"

"I give up. Ella faxed over a list of her belongings she wants shipped!" Romano blurted, accepting his coffee from a maid.

"I can't wait!" Allison squealed.

Tomas had joined Mike Connelly outside on the black driveway, standing next to the silver Jaguar. Mike said, "There is a meeting this afternoon!"

"Regarding Ella-Louisa?" Tomas asked.

"No way Don will want to live in England."

"I think that lord guy would have his own security?" Tomas said.

Mike looked at him. "I don't think he has…."

"Draw straws?"

"No. Miss Alice will have to employ someone English! And I just know who that is!" Mike said.

****

Harlsby-Hall - Harlsby - 11th July 2006 - 11.00 a.m.

"Miss Ella, visitor," the theatrical voice from Andrews sounded.

"Thank you, Andrews. Please send them through to the drawing room." Ella said while she continued to open the acceptance letters from the morning post.

Removing herself from the nineteenth century oak library, Ella walked towards the sitting room. Opening the creaking door, she found a strange, muscular, dark-haired man.

"May I be of any help?" Ella smiled with her bright red lipstick grin.

"Miss Ella, my name is Mark Barker. I am your new security officer."

"What about Don Spelling?" she replied, confused.

"Don is flying back to the states."

"Why? Is he being extradited? Not that he did anything wrong, I mean…"

"The only thing he did wrong was leaving you," he smiled, still standing in the centre of the dark oak drawing room.

"You look familiar."

Mark smiled. "Yes, my brother Matty is Benedict's security officer."

“Please, sit down.” Ella forgot her manners and walked over to a green leather Chesterfield chair and placed herself into it.

Taking his seat on the Chesterfield sofa Mark continued, “We are twins. You will find that we are very similar. My brother is here in Harlsby!”

“With Benedict?” Ella commented in confusion.

A towering male burst into the room.

Benedict!” she hollered. “You frightened me. What are you doing here?”

“I’m in the UK in two tournaments. I have a couple of days free.”

“Where is your coach?”

“London.”

“I don’t understand,” Ella puffed.

Benedict walked over to her bodyguard and high fived him. “Pen!”

“What about her?”

Penelope Tomkinson-Clifton paced into the vast drawing room. “Ben!”

Benedict sat down on the vacant sofa, and Penelope placed herself next to him.

“Are you two...” Ella said, moving her finger in between the two of them.

Benedict laughed. "No, just good friends."

"Oh, I see," Ella whispered.

Penelope Tomkinson-Clifton was nineteen years old, dark haired and of a medium skin tone. Her eyes were a piercing blue. She resembled her brother Dickie.

"I love someone else," she said, thumping Benedict's huge arm.

"Does…"

"Yes, Dickie knows. It was his idea," Penelope said.

"Rup's wedding. Nat and Angel. You and Dickie. Pen and Andy." Benedict said, but never mentioned himself.

"Andy? …

"Andy La-Mount-Martinez…" Benedict laughed.

"Anyway, I'm too busy winning my championships to marry. I have two VIP tickets to the Rona Cup Championships next Sunday in Basildon." Benedict leaned over and passed Ella a white envelope. "Please come, sis!"

"Who are you playing?" Ella said. "Would you like tea?"

Both declined. Benedict continued, "Lee S. Marconi."

"It's always Lee S. Marconi and Ben Mancini in the finals," Penelope huffed.

"You are in the finals?" Ella asked.

"Yes, I have been playing all week! I'm back tomorrow, six-hour practise sessions!" Benedict said.

"I thought you had a couple of days off!"

"I did. I spent all day with Pen and Andy in her flat yesterday and today I thought I would see my sis."

"So, Andy is in London?"

"Yes, he's in the gallery today. Mom is coming to the match with Sebastian and Oliver!" Benedict said with his cheeky grin.

"I knew she was flying over. I suppose they will remain here until after the wedding." Ella gave a precautious look.

"Dad's flying over nearer to the wedding with Seb, Sarah-Jane, Rup, and Rachel."

"That's not good. She will be heavily pregnant!" gasped Ella.

"Maxi and Davis are flying too."

"Belinda, Lucinda?" Ella asked

"The girls are flying in early and hitting London, staying at Seb's."

"Oh my God!" Ella whispered again.

"Nat is staying here?" Penelope cut in.

"It's his wedding too!"

CHAPTER 10

NYC International Airport - New York

20th July 2006 - 9.00 a.m.

Oliver Dupont paced, gripping his mobile phone. The VIP private area remained calm as he growled to his editors.

Sebastian huffed, “Darling, I really do not understand what’s wrong!”

Allison gripped her head with both hands and placed both elbows onto her knees. “I can’t get rid of this headache!”

“Is it that dreadful woman thing?” Sebastian replied, drinking his tea from a porcelain cup.

“Menopause.” Allison answered.

“That is not going to do your headache much good, is it?” Sebastian gestured.

Oliver walked over to the brown leather sofa, wearing dark blue contour jeans, pale blue dress shirt and a Sylvester–Montgomery double breasted navy jacket.

Sebastian looked at him in amusement. “Are you over your tantrum?”

“Something I organised didn’t work out,” Oliver sighed.

Sebastian patted the seat next to him. “Sit. The whole business will be finished soon.”

Oliver sat. “Just a few hiccups.”

Allison stared at the pair of them, wondering what the hell they were talking about, when suddenly an explosion of vomit hit the royal blue carpet.

Sebastian and Tomas jumped up instantly and called for help. Oliver rushed over to where Allison was sitting, avoiding the congealed breakfast splattered on the floor.

"Alice, you, okay?" Oliver said, gripping the pale female in his arms.

A medic approached the sickly superstar, and Tomas intervened while Oliver smiled, moving away from her.

"Can I examine her?" He asked Allison's bodyguard.

Tomas acknowledged the medic dressed in his navy NYC International tailored suit. Allowing him to pass, the medic approached Allison.

"How are you feeling?" he said, sitting next to her, opening his medical bag.

Allison just nodded. "I have a bad headache, and sometimes I throw up with the pain. In fact, I feel much better now!"

Sebastian and Oliver shrugged their shoulders and glanced at each other while the medic checked her blood pressure and temperature.

"She will be okay to fly," he said.

"Thank you," Oliver stepped in.

“Alice, are you feeling better?” Sebastian asked the superstar.

“One hundred percent,”

The Mancini jet was ready to board. Two well-dressed male attendants accompanied the superstar and her three merry men. Sebastian was getting a little hot under the collar with the beautiful sight that strolled with them.

Climbing the airstair onto the Mancini 757, Sebastian asked one of the gorgeous attendants for assistance. His blood pressure had escalated to boiling point.

Allison looked up at the sky while Tomas chuckled behind her. Looking flustered, Sebastian breathed in fresh air before stepping inside the jet. Oliver had to wipe his eyes with laughter.

Sebastian took his place on a cream leather recliner and thanked the young man for his help. Oliver followed his beloved and placed himself directly across from him. Allison was already seated behind the couple and asked a steward when brunch would be served.

Turning around from his elegant leather seat, Sebastian said, “Alice, are you hungry?”

“I’m starved!” she replied, popping a pill. “Remember, my breakfast is all over the carpet!”

Sebastian stared at Oliver in disgust. "Oh yes, I remember!" he whispered, placing his handkerchief against his nostrils.

****

The Rona Cup Tennis Championships

Basildon - Essex

23rd July 2006 - 2.00 p.m.

The grass court bathed in the richness of the summer sun. Allison Templeton-Mancini sported a Sylvester-Montgomery cream flared suit and straw brim hat. Drinking champagne, she giggled. "Sebastian, isn't it strange to have a floating strawberry in your drink?"

Sebastian Dupont looked every inch the perfect Englishman. Wearing his light grey suit and purple cravat, he smiled. "Darling Alice, would you prefer that it sink?"

The championship's hospitality was located within the grounds of the twelve grass tennis courts. Situated in a stunning landscape garden next to court one, the organisers greeted Allison, Sebastian, Oliver, Penelope, Andrew La-Mount-Martinez, Ella-Louisa, and Dickie.

Directing the seven VIPs to a private area with fine dining and afternoon tea, Allison's security remained segregated and relaxed within an informal lounge.

Oliver, sporting a grey morning suit, embraced the atmosphere, taking photographs with his mobile phone.

Sebastian observed his workaholic husband and grinned with pride.

"Uncle Sebastian, why is Oliver always working?" Ella-Louisa said, gripping her purple wide brim sun hat.

"Well, I am now retired, a house husband and Oliver prefers to work!" he smiled, taking a sip of champagne.

Ella-Louisa, wearing a pale lilac flowered long maxi dress and bolero jacket, looked stunning. "Oh, I see…." she replied, grabbing another glass of champagne from the waiter.

"Ella, are you not warm with gloves?" Allison asked

"No, Mom, they are lace!"

"I was going to wear purple," Allison scoffed from under her wide straw hat. Revealing her pale features and bright red lipstick, she said, "I thought of the English countryside, straw!"

"I'm wearing purple," Sebastian chipped in, placing his hand on his cravat. "Regal!"

A deep, polite voice interrupted the conversation. "Sir, we must escort you to the Royal Box."

"Royal Box?" Allison whispered.

"Yes, Marquess of Harlsby. Mom!" Ella jumped in.

"I knew I should have worn purple!" Allison moaned again.

Penelope, dressed in a pale green sun dress and jacket, held onto Ella's arm while they both giggled, following Dickie.

Sebastian, Oliver, and Allison were escorted separately. Walking through the main entrance of the pergola into the main restaurant, other dignitaries stopped and stared. The superstar and her friends ignored their whispers and walked towards a set of green doors.

Allison could hear 'It's Allison Templeton-Mancini. Oh my God, that's *Conception's* boss, Oliver. Sebastian Dupont!'

Climbing a set of purple-carpeted steps, powerful rays of sunlight hit Allison as a warm, sultry breeze blew her hat. An official guided the three VIPs to a set of lilac chairs on the first row of the Royal Box.

Sitting next to her daughter, she heard the crowd applaud. Standing up from her seat, she waved to the 10,000 spectators sitting inside the oval stadium.

Placing herself back down into her seat, she hid behind her large Sylvester sunglasses.

A familiar voice echoed behind. "You look gorgeous in that design, darling!"

"Miles!" Allison laughed, turning around.

Fabian-Astor-Sylvester and Miles Montgomery smiled. Wearing grape morning suits and iris cravats, they agreed the cut was perfect for her.

Ella-Louisa commented, “Fabian, Miles, Mom looks beautiful in her suit.”

“That is the idea! What are you wearing, my baby girl?” Fabian said, browsing his eyes against Ella’s dress.

“Charles-Montgomery!”

Miles burst into laughter. “My father’s design…”

“Why didn’t you ask me?” Fabian projected.

“I didn’t have the time, and I found an old dress from years ago in regal colours and…”

Fabian lifted his hand up. “Enough!”

More people invaded the Royal Box taking their places, in awe of the superstar her guests. The crowds applauded a baseball-capped male stepping out onto the court, carrying a huge bag.

Sebastian leaned towards Ella. “Who is that?”

Ella replied, “Lee S. Marconi, Ben’s rival. Real name, Leon-Sean!”

“Oh, I see. He looks different today.” Sebastian commented.

“Its outdoors. The last time we watched him play he was indoors.” Oliver said.

"Oh, that is why is baggage is huge!" Sebastian mumbled.

A booming roar escalated around the stadium as Benedict Templeton-Mancini walked out onto the court, wearing his ear buds and plated hair. The six-foot-two pin-up smiled and waved to the crowd.

Seeing his mother in the Royal Box, he nodded and placed his bag down next to his seat. Lee S. Marconi, also from the US, replaced his cap with a white hairband and walked into the centre of the court and waved.

Benedict removed his white hoodie and unzipped his bag. Selecting a racket, Benedict walked over to the baseline where a green-clad ball boy rolled two balls towards him. Winking at the boy, he picked up the balls and began his ten-minute warm up.

The umpire greeted both players at the net and tossed a coin. Benedict won the toss and selected to serve first, facing the Royal Box. Lee S. Marconi scowled at Benedict and stormed to the opposite base line.

The crowd fell silent when the players had taken their positions. Benedict served his first ace: the ball popped, and Marconi just couldn't reach it in time.

Allison applauded.

Ella-Louisa said, "He's so powerful!"

"Like your father!" Allison replied.

Ella looked bemused at her mother.

Benedict continued to fire drop shots, forehand, and lobs. First game, Mancini. Marconi fought back to take the second game but couldn't overcome his defeated service break in the fourth. Benedict won the first set, 6-1.

Taking a drink of bottled water, Benedict noticed Marconi complaining to the umpire. The twenty-one-year-old American blonde wasn't happy with the late calls.

Benedict knew this was his weakness, and he nodded towards his coaches near the VIP box. Sebastian watched with anticipation. "Lots of nodding and winking," he whispered to Oliver.

"That Marconi guy is becoming weak. You watch!" Oliver grinned.

The players walked back onto the court. Marconi served first. Every hit, swing, and drop, Marconi screamed. The umpire at one stage had to remind Mr Marconi to calm down.

"Why is he making so much noise?" Allison said.

"He's trying to put Ben off!" Ella replied.

"Cheating," Allison huffed.

Ella-Louisa laughed. "Mom says Marconi is a cheat!"

"He is, our Ben will thrash him!" Penelope replied, holding Andrew's hand.

Benedict continued to break his serve: second set, Mancini. An official walked onto the court carrying a medical bag. Benedict looked at his coaches and shrugged.

"What's wrong now?" Allison winced.

"He's hurt!" Fabian replied from behind.

Allison turned around. "His pride's hurt!"

"Correct!" Fabian grinned.

"I'm bored with this play acting!" Allison moaned. "I need tea."

"But what brand?" Sebastian joked.

Allison, Miles, and Sebastian all progressed to the hospitality gardens for afternoon tea. She couldn't stand the atrocious acting from a wannabe tennis star. Sitting on an exquisite rattan cushioned sofa, sheltered by a huge lilac sun brolly, drinking Earl Grey tea in china cups was sheer bliss.

"Marvellous tea!" Miles said.

"You know, British designers like yourself and your father made the opening for other designers to break through." Allison said, drinking her tea.

"My father?" Miles said.

"Charles! My mama was the face of Montgomery!"

Miles smiled. "Ella-Louisa is the face of Sylvester-Montgomery!"

“Yes….” Allison sighed. “I remember when I was the face of The House of Sylvester. My first day here in London, all those years ago.”

“I remember that day very well. I was Alice’s PA!” Sebastian grinned.

“Really? I just know that you guys are a double act,” laughed Miles.

“Friends for life!!” Sebastian and Allison shouted.

The cheers of the crowd erupted into whistles.

“I believe they may have finished their match. Best go and see!” Sebastian said.

The three VIPs made their way back to their seats and the match was over. Benedict Templeton-Mancini had won the title at the age of nineteen. Allison applauded and blew him a kiss, while crowds of fans jumped hysterically.

Officials walked out onto the court, carrying a magnificent silver trophy. The ball girls and boys lined up against the baseline and the umpire waited beside the two contestants. A microphone was placed in the centre of the court whilst TV crews and journalists were positioned in their media area.

A spokesperson began to wander around the court, speaking to the crowd with another official waiting to hand over the trophy. The runner up, Marconi, paced towards the official and grabbed his small silver plate, disgusted. Benedict tried not to laugh.

The official announced Benedict the 2006 Rona Cup Champion. Screams, cheers, and whistles bellowed into the atmosphere. Benedict walked towards the official and accepted the polished silver cup. Holding it into the air, he walked around the court, displaying it to the crowds. Having his photograph taken and thanking the officials, Benedict faced the Royal Box and bowed to his mother.

****

Shower products, deodorants and moisturisers stood in wicker baskets between marble pillars. Stripping off his sodden perspired t-shirt, Benedict breathed a sigh of relief. Sitting on a polished oak bench, he untied his long black hair and allowed it to fall over his shoulders. His pectoralis muscles flexed against his movements while his long anterior upper leg muscles relaxed against the cotton fabric of his white shorts.

Out of the corner of his eye, he saw a tall figure lurking near the timber faced lockers. Stretching out his olive tanned legs, he said, “Come on out, spoilt brat!”

Lee S. Marconi walked over towards him, holding both hands in surrender. “Okay, big guy. You got me!”

“What’s happening, man?” Benedict laughed.

“I miss you,” Lee replied, looking down at the tiled floor.

"Me too." Benedict grabbed Lee's hand.

"I hate all of this. The cover up, the deceit."

"Deceit?" Benedict answered. "Don't kid yourself. Everybody knows how the game is played."

"What about Pen?"

"She is forever pushing me. Wants you to stay in London with us. I haven't told her the full story, until Mom knows the score." Benedict whispered, "I told Ella!"

"Ben, how did Ella react?" Lee said, concerned.

Benedict laughed. "Well enough to invite you to the wedding."

"Really?" Lee responded, placing a kiss on Benedict's moist lips. "I love you Mancini."

****

Matty Barker leaned against the changing room door. Guarding the lovers was part of his security agreement. An official walked up to him with a clipboard. Wearing the official club's attire, he motioned forward towards Matty.

"Is it possible if you could let me through, please?" said the Englishman.

"I'm afraid not. Mr Mancini has requested time alone."

"Oh, I see. I am required to escort Mr Mancini to the club's hospitality room. His family are waiting," the British male said.

Towering above him, Matty refused to flinch. "Wait here."

Matty walked into the changing room. The aromas of sex and shampoo intermingled in the steam. Coughing, he said, "Ben, I'm sorry to interrupt, but the officials need you in the family room."

Benedict appeared from the steam wearing just a towel. "Okay, good with me. Give me five."

Matty nodded and wondered if the steam had eaten Lee. It was quiet until a voice sounded. "Come and scrub my back!"

****

Penelope, Dickie, and Ella-Louisa relaxed in the family area in the main building, surrounded by extravagant people and luxurious furnishings. Drinking champagne and Earl Grey, Penelope squealed. "Ben!"

Dickie laughed. "Number one fan!"

Ella-Louisa laughed, "Yes, Pen loves Ben. Besties!" Ella knew Benedict was truly in love with Lee. Finding out all about him was going to be her next challenge.

****

Harlsby-Hall - Harlsby - 23rd July 2006 - 8.00 p.m.

Stretched out upon an elegant oak four-poster bed, Allison dabbed her forehead with a damp facecloth. Placing the willow-patterned wash basin down onto the bed covers, she inclined against her soft, fluffy pillows. Understanding that her hot flashes were getting worse, Allison unbuttoned her silk cream blouse.

Benedict had achieved his goal today by winning The Rona Cup Tennis Championships, and she wasn't going to upset anyone, especially her youngest child.

A knock sounded at the bedroom door. Buttoning her blouse and placing the basin beneath her bed, she ran her fingers over her skirt.

"Come in!" she voiced.

"Mom!" Ella-Louisa said, pacing into her room.

"Whatever is the matter?"

Benedict followed, closing the door behind him. Allison laughed. "A visit from my two youngest!"

Benedict flopped onto the bed wearing an open neck dress shirt and black tailored trousers. Ella joined her brother, wearing a black off the shoulder dinner dress.

"Mom!" Ella stared at her mother still not dressed for dinner.

Allison took her place in a velvet relaxer chair opposite her children. "Spill the beans!"

"It's Pen," Ella-Louisa said.

Allison shrugged. "What about her?"

"She proposed!" Ella announced in despair.

"I wasn't aware that the two of you were together, Benedict!" Allison misinterprets Ella's news.

"Not me. I'm gay!" Benedict fell into silence and looked down at the bedspread.

Allison grinned at her beloved son stretched out, covering his deep brown eyes.

"I know. I have always known," Allison smiled.

"You have?" Benedict jumped up. "How?"

"A mother's knowledge."

"I cannot tell anyone, or my career will be ruined!"

"We are in the twenty-first century, Benedict. Are you in love with someone?" Allison relaxed further back into the armchair.

"Leon!" Ella chipped in. "Pen loves Andy-La-Mount-Martinez!"

Allison remained confused. "The spoilt tennis player?"

"Yep," Benedict replied, staring at his mother. "It's all an act. Marconi and Mancini. One a good guy, the other the bad guy!"

"Oh," Allison whispered. "How long?"

"A year," Benedict explained. "I fell in love with him in Australia."

"Dickie is shocked regarding Andy, he thought Pen loved Ben!" Ella cut in again.

Allison puffed a sigh of relief. "Women shouldn't throw themselves at men!"

"That is what Dickie is saying!" Ella agreed with her mother on that score.

Allison stood up from her seat and walked shoeless across the burgundy-coloured carpet. "Don't worry, it won't leave this room."

Benedict said. "My bros already know, and Lee is escorting me to the wedding. But Dad is in the dark."

"This will kill your father," Allison whispered, looking at her children.

CHAPTER 11

Harlsby-Hall - Harlsby - 5th August 2006 - 11.00 a.m.

Entering the light-filled hallway with its bohemian history, wedding coordinators spoke into their radios and ticked their wooden clipboards with expensive pens.

Outside loomed dark cumulonimbus clouds, levitating above the abandoned landscape. Four immense brilliant white marquees stood below the threating sky. Staff walked into the marquees, wearing Victorian servant uniforms in black and white. Each member supported a sash of blue and yellow, displaying a serpent's head on a coat of arms.

Allison held Fabian's hand and wept into her tissue while she observed the activity outside. Turning around from the sash bedroom window, she muttered, "You look beautiful, Ella."

Ella-Louisa glanced at herself in the silver dress mirror. The bead-covered full-length white gown sparkled the hand-sewn sequins against the natural daylight. The short sleeves and round neckline screamed - the roaring twenties.

Refusing to wear a veil, Ella-Louisa dazzled in a diamond feather flapper headband. Her pale skin radiated against brilliant red lipstick and dark raven hair. Creating a finger wave up-do, she looked the part. Selecting her white lace gloves and lily of the valley posy, Ella was ready to become the Marchioness of Harlsby.

Fabian agreed Ella was magnificent while he tutted at Allison. "My darling Alice, you are gaining weight!"

"Rubbish. I'm fine!" she giggled, looking at herself in the mirror. Behind her mask she would agree with Fabian. Her breasts were already a size larger, at which Romano was very impressed.

"Mom, you look beautiful," Ella beamed, opening the door for the photographers.

Conception Magazine and *Mayfair Recount* were the selected magazines to seize the exclusives. Oliver Dupont, wearing an exquisite navy-blue morning suit, burst into the room. "Ella, you look beautiful."

"What about me?" Allison coughed.

Oliver laughed. "You always look a million dollars!"

"That bad, huh?" she said.

****

"Come on, get a move on!" Rupert said.

"I have a dead arm!" Nathaniel moaned.

Behind the floral screen, Nathaniel struggled to tie his red cravat. Standing in a red waistcoat, his best man continued to punch him.

A knock sounded at the door and Allison walked in. "What is going on behind that screen?".

Nathaniel popped his head up and looked over the top. "Tell Rup to stop hitting me!"

Rupert bent his head around the side of the screen. “Hi, mom, he’s just struggling with his tie.”

“He’s strangling me!” Nathaniel yelled.

“Let me!” Allison said, walking around the screen. Taking the loose fabric into her dainty fingers, Allison began to tie the cravat. “You two look like your father.”

“Is that a good thing?” Nathaniel grinned.

****

Miles and Bartholomew Montgomery placed the three-meter cathedral veil upon Angel’s head. The crystals twinkled against her auburn curls that cascaded down her ivory backless fishtail dress.

Angel held her bouquet of white roses, while she observed the diamante dress. “Perfect!” Bartholomew said.

Allison knocked and walked into the room. “Oh, Angel, you look beautiful.”

Angel smiled in the mirror towards Allison. “Thank you, Alice!”

“Alice, darling! You look wonderful in the dress.” Miles smiled.

“You, me, Bart, and Fabian look like we have just stepped out of Wonderland!” she laughed.

“Purple,” Bartholomew smiled, standing in his iris morning suit. “The up-and-coming colour!”

“Does Romano like the red and purple striped design?” Miles commented.

“He does,” Allison chuckled. “I believe he likes the purple swirls on his waistcoat.”

Removing herself from the deep maroon Victorian bedroom, Allison made her way down the curved staircase. Suddenly she spotted her youngest son Benedict, hiding behind a lacquered pillar.

“Benedict!” called Allison, pacing towards the tall raven-haired male.

“I love you,” he whispered, holding onto Lee’s jacket.

“Leon!” Allison presumed.

“Yes?” Benedict smirked.

“Mrs Templeton-Mancini, my pleasure.” Lee bowed. Dressed in a navy morning suit and pale blue waistcoat, Lee S. Marconi showed off his personable style.

“Leon, pleased to meet you.” Allison beamed at the blonde tennis player.

“Don’t worry about dad. He knows.” Benedict released Leon’s hand.

Allison became pale. “Really?”

“Hit it off with Lee, really loves him!” Benedict blushed.

Leon turned towards Allison. “Mrs...”

Allison held her left hand up. “Call me Alice, Leon.”

****

Penelope's dark hair remained wedged against a diamante bun. Dressed in her lavender 1920s bridesmaid dress, she smiled at Ella-Louisa.

"I lost my virginity last night!" Penelope's voice echoed around the deep hardwood bedroom.

Ella glanced across at her as she waited for her father to arrive. It was stressful enough enduring an hour long photo session with your designers and parents, but this aggravated her even more.

"We are talking about Andy," Ella muttered in shock.

"Andy La-Mount-Martinez?" Penelope laughed.

"Pen!" Ella cried out.

"He loves me. I couldn't wait. We're still getting married!"

"But doesn't he stay at your apartment in London?

"Yes, we do stuff, but not the full thing." she grinned.

Ella looked up at the ceiling and continued to sit in the maroon traditional armchair, pulling her face with uncertainty.

"I'm flying to New York the day after tomorrow!" Penelope broke in.

"Have you met Lucinda and Max?"

Squealing, "Yes, they are great and I'm not coming back!"

Horror hit Ella. Her grandmama had done the same thing. History was repeating itself. Lady Eleanor Templeton-Jones had run away with Theo-James Miller to Los Angeles in 1938. Viscount Templeton had repudiated his only daughter.

"You can't!" Ella stepped in.

"Why?"

"You'll need a visa!" Ella was trying to make excuses.

"I have one! Andy is sorting me a work visa while I live with him."

"In Manhattan?"

Penelope stood up and walked over from the bed. Bending down to Ella-Louisa, she said, "I'm going to work for David in the *Galleria.* Andy and I are marrying on the 6th of September in Manhattan. It is going to be a quiet ceremony, and I want you and Dickie to be there."

"Dickie doesn't know?" Ella stared at Penelope.

"He will."

"Oh my God," Ella whispered. "You are going to start a war!"

"All is fair in love and war," Penelope beamed.

Ella looked towards her sister-in-law. "You must tell Dickie. I always thought you were in love with Ben!"

Penelope replied, “We are like brother and sister!”

Romano Mancini strolled into the room, wearing his black morning suit, red and purple striped cravat and matching waistcoat. “I heard there was a war.”

****

Harlsby Family Chapel - 12.30 p.m.

Yew trees swayed against the humid breeze, concealing the grey stone chapel from view. Allison chatted with Belinda outside the wrought iron gates. Lighting her cigarette, the redhead soap star observed the area.

Leaning in, Belinda, wearing a green plunged-neck gown, whispered, “That guy over there. He groped me!”

Allison pointed in the direction towards a grey-haired male. “You mean Lord Towersand?”

“Gramps? He’s a lord! Touched my arse!” She inhaled a mouthful of tobacco.

Allison collapsed laughing “You could be a lady!”

Belinda muttered between blows. “I’ll be dead!

“What age do you think he is?” Allison sniggered with laughter.

“Ninety!” Belinda observed the grinning male, winking at her.

“Just take out some life insurance!” Allison’s tears fell onto her cheeks.

Sebastian Templeton-Mancini strolled up to the pair holding his wife's delicate hand. "Okay, Belinda, you've set mom off!" he grinned.

"Mom!" Sarah-Jane smirked.

"I'm pointing out the facts, darling." Belinda motioned towards her daughter.

"Dad won't be happy that you are smoking again," Sarah-Jane implied.

"Neither am I!" said Belinda, stomping out her cigarette butt with green stilettos.

Sebastian kissed his mother's hand and commented on her flushed appearance. Nathaniel, Benedict, and Rupert had also gathered.

"My God! The four Romanos." Belinda grinned.

Allison leaned into Nathaniel and Rupert. "Where is Rachel?"

"Rach is with Jake and Helen," Rupert cut in.

"Remember, she is heavily pregnant!" Allison said concerningly.

"She is actually talking to Uncle Richard and Henry," Nathaniel joined the conversation.

"Whatever. Make sure she is okay!"

Two vintage cream-coloured Rolls Royces pulled up outside the chapel.

“Nathaniel, go!” Allison screamed.

Two photographers took their positions while chauffeurs opened the rear passenger doors. Belinda and the boys disappeared into the chapel.

Romano climbed out and held his hand for Ella to grip. Placing herself onto the gravelled track, she looked stunning in the daylight.

Fay-Elizabeth Pullman stepped out of the first car wearing a red satin princess dress. Gripping onto her small posy of white roses, she waved at Allison. Following Fay stepped out Penelope in her lavish lavender dress, holding a white rose posy.

Approaching the chapel gates, parking behind the second Rolls Royce, a red vintage limousine. Theatre Director Charles Medley-Garrett strode out from the rear passenger door, looking stunning in his grey morning suit. His appearance resembled something from the Victorian period with his cropped hair and beard.

Angel stepped out in her figure-hugging backless fishtail dress and flowing cathedral veil. Allison walked over to both brides and kissed them on their blushed cheeks. Placing a kiss on Romano’s lips, she took her position in the chapel doorway.

Allison walked down the small aisle with Fay. Following them were Angel and her father Charles. Romano and Ella-Louisa followed last, with Penelope in front.

The ceremony sailed smoothly, apart from Nathaniel crying when he said his vows. Allison scrambled towards the couple standing at the altar and passed him a tissue. Taking her place again, in the hundred-year-old pew, Romano gripped her hand tight.

The intense headache she had endeavoured to surpass began to appear again. Still gripping onto Romano, she breathed a sigh of relief when the vicar announced, "husband and wife."

Walking into the vestry to sign the register, the new marchioness noticed her mother becoming red. "Mom, do you want a drink of water?"

Allison nodded while Ella-Louisa asked the vicar if her mother could have a glass of water. Romano continued to watch Nathaniel and Angel pose for photographs next to the register while Allison choked down an aspirin.

"You alright, Alice?" Dickie asked, holding onto his new wife's hand.

"I'm great. It's your turn to sign," she spoke.

Completing her photographs with both Ella and Nathaniel's signings, Allison disappeared. She found a bathroom in the vicar's office. Vomiting into the toilet, she sat on the floor and leaned against the door. Drying her lips with a tissue, she struggled to stand up.

A knock sounded behind her, and a smart English accent whispered, "Mrs Templeton-Mancini, may I inquire if you are all right?"

Allison slumped. "Yes," she mumbled, trying not to ruin her children's big day. Back against the door, she managed to pull herself up. Removing her compact mirror from her mauve clutch bag, she painted her dry lips with brilliant red lipstick.

Opening the door and breathing in, she smiled at the curate. "Too much water!"

The curate smiled. "Yes, it is a very muggy day."

"I feel much better," she said, continuing to walk towards the vestry.

Romano grabbed Allison's hand and followed the two bridal processions into the cool chapel.

"I should be walking with Charles," she whispered.

"No, you are staying by my side. We are going to have a chat later." Romano said, through his gritted teeth.

Outside the chapel, Allison put on her round sunglasses. Even though the day was dull, the bright light aggravated Allison's eyes. Romano hung onto his wife while the photographers yelled out their instructions.

Belinda and Lucinda ran up to Allison and asked Romano to relieve his wife. Refusing two of his dearest friends, he walked Allison towards the marquee after the photographers had finished.

"What the hell are you doing, Romano?" Allison glared at him.

Romano turned and stared at her, standing still on the shamrock-green lawn, and holding Allison in his clutches, he said, "Something is going on!"

"I don't understand!" she barked.

"You are not well, and you are trying to avoid me! I have heard you in the mornings vomiting!"

"You think I'm pregnant!"

"No!"

"Eating disorder!" Allison scoffed, immediately she burst into tears.

Gripping her tightly and pulling her hard into his chest Romano shushed her. "It's okay, baby, don't cry…."

"I can't spoil our children's wedding's." She dribbled into Romano's waistcoat.

"I'm booking you into Maxi's clinic again. You urgently need help. You are not leaving my side Allison Templeton-Mancini. Ever!

****

The glamourous reception of both couples ran into the late evening. Allison supplied herself with more champagne and relaxed with the clique and Romano. Sebastian and Oliver Dupont enjoyed the celebrity guests of royalty, while Amile Templeton-Miller attracted the attention of Viscount Ludwig Baldwin, who had fallen head over heels in love with her.

Belinda complained to her husband Donny Davis that a dirty old lord was stalking her. Lucinda observed her son Andrew and his new love Penelope constantly disappearing. Allison watched her son's gathered by the bar, gossiping over bottled beers. "This is perfect" she thought.

Smiling at Romano she whispered, "Come on, let's go and make love."

"I love making up!" He grinned moving his eyebrows up and down.

The superstar and her husband bid their farewells and retired to their luxury Victorian bedroom. Making love until the early morning they both fell deeply into sleep, cuddled into one – always.

****

Harlsby-Hall - Harlsby - 6th August 2006 - 9.30 a.m.

Birds chirped against the morning rays. Hills and tracks created shadows against the countryside horizon. Trackers and farmers ploughed against a backdrop of brown soil and yellow rape.

“Good morning!” said Sebastian.

“Morning,” grunted Belinda behind dark sunglasses.

“Morning, B,” laughed Oliver, taking his place across from her.

Two uniformed males strolled towards Sebastian and Oliver. “Would you care for hot beverages?”

“Earl Grey and black coffee, please.” Sebastian said.

“Excuse me, could I have another Bloody Mary with egg!” Belinda said.

“Bad head?” Oliver said.

“No, Donny says I’m the best, of course I have a bad head.” Belinda scowled.

The forty-seater white linen table prepared for a lavish banquet hosted most of its guests. The aroma of bacon, sausage, fresh bread, and fruit captured Oliver’s nostrils.

The Templeton-Miller siblings and their spouses strolled into the historic dining room, where huge canvases of the marquess’s ancestors hung in pride.

“Morning everyone!” Henry smiled, sitting next to Oliver.

“Morning!” everyone replied, apart from Belinda, who gestured with her hand.

Ricky Brown-Templeton-Miller took his place next to Sebastian and said, "Did you think my sis looked ill yesterday?"

Annie Brown-Templeton-Miller, Donny Davis, Ami, and Richard Templeton-Miller agreed. Sebastian remained quiet while accepting his Earl Grey tea. Pouring the contents into his china cup, he remarked, "Alice is overdoing it!"

"Romano will keep an eye on her," Oliver smiled.

Lucinda, Max, and Andrew La-Mount-Martinez walked into the room. "I'm starved!" Andrew announced.

"Sex-starved," Belinda muttered under her breath.

"Where is David?" Sebastian asked, selecting his lemon.

"In bed with my daughter!" Henry piped up. "When are they going to get married?"

Rene looked at her husband and patted his hand. "They will marry when the time is right."

"No rush!" Sebastian agreed.

****

Maroon and green striped drapes sealed the outside light from the depths of Allison's and Romano's bedroom. Cuddled up under the huge mass of duvet, the couple began to move.

"This bed is too small. I ache all over," Romano muttered. "You awake, baby?"

"I am now!" she groaned.

A knock at the door startled Romano. Jumping out of the bed naked, he paced towards the oak door. Opening the wooden structure, peeping between the crack, he answered. "Yeah!"

"The Marquess and Marchioness have sent breakfast, sir," the English voice announced.

"Leave it on the floor, please," Romano replied, covering his genitals with his spare hand.

Once the sound of the tray hit the floor and footsteps grew quieter, Romano poked his head out. Remaining naked, he pulled the tray inside the room and locked the door.

"Breakfast. Shall I open the drapes?" he asked.

"Let me get my robe," Allison said, removing herself from the pastel-coloured sheet and walking over to the brass hook behind the door.

Romano placed the tray down onto the bed and opened the heavy drapes. "Sun came for breakfast, too," he smiled.

Allison climbed back into bed and reached for the Earl Grey. Unbottling two aspirin, she poured the tea into a white china cup.

Romano poured his cafetiere coffee into a mug and smelled the aroma. Caressing Allison's bare breast underneath her robe, he said, "You need a bigger cup."

"Nah, it's espresso," smirked Allison, untying her robe.

“This is so cool, eating breakfast naked!” Romano laid on his side, nibbling scrambled eggs atop a slice of brown toast.

“You’re just horny!” Allison laughed, admiring Romano’s body.

“Espresso, huh,” he grinned.

Opening her legs wide, Allison laughed. “Maybe!”

“Come here, baby!” moaned Romano.

The tray fell from the bed, and Romano rolled on top of Allison. Feeling his arousal, Allison moaned with ecstasy while Romano kissed every centimetre of her soft, soothing skin.

Romano couldn’t wait and felt his way within her moist sex. Pushing himself forward, deeper into her, he moved himself into position and paced himself rhythmically with Allison. Both panted and groaned within their boundaries. She let out a light scream of pleasure while Romano grunted into the bedding.

Slowing down, Romano sighed. Allison breathed hard and had to pull Romano from the top of her. Running to the bathroom, she needed to pee. Romano followed her into the bathroom and watched in confusion.

Grabbing at tissue, she laughed, “I will be wearing diapers soon.” Looking at her naked husband propped against the door. “I’m good. I feel better!”

Romano stared. “Is your bladder weak?”

“Menopause. I’m getting old!”

“Baby! You’re not getting old. It’s…”

“Tea?” she insisted.

“Let’s make that call today… Maxi Spink be ready for the Mancinis.

CHAPTER 12

Montrose Gatehouse III - Mayfair - London

7th August 2006 - 1.00 p.m.

Miles Peterson leaned against the white gloss island, observing the rain splashing against the window through the venetian blinds.

"Jonathan, I have noticed the final transfer from Germany," Miles spoke, while the bright light from his opened laptop reflected upon his black-framed spectacles.

Jonathan smirked against his home office desk in New York. "Good, we can close Germany!"

"Do it," Miles instructed.

"Just two more, Miami and here!" Jonathan grinned.

"So, cash-wise?" Miles asked.

"Two billion for me, two billion for you, two billion for JP, and two billion for Mr D."

"The rest?" Miles cleared his throat.

"Twenty-five million for Sandy Hill, one million for security, twenty-five grand for workers.

"What about MD?" Miles cut in.

"Two billion." Jonathan said.

"Nice and even. Freidman hasn't got a clue."

"Stage three next?" Jonathan said.

“Wait for my go-ahead,” Miles said, looking out the waterlogged window.

Calling off, Miles strolled towards Hillary’s office. Knocking at her door, he called, “May I come in?”

“Yes,” she replied, sitting at her desk with her paperwork. “Do you ever get fed up with the cold?”

“Why? The cold is never fed up with me.”

Miles’s white smile lit the room. “I love you, Jonah!”

“I love you too, Peterson!”

“Coffee?”

The doorbell rang, and Miles pressed the security button to release the gate. “They’re here!”

Jake, Helen, and Fay Pullman were removing their overnight cases from the polished BMW they had hired for the wedding vacation at Harlsby-Hall.

“How did all go?” Miles gestured towards the house.

“Beautiful,” Helen said, kissing Miles on his cheek.

“I bet you looked beautiful in your dress, Princess Fay,” Miles grinned.

Fay high fived him and followed her mother inside. Jake hugged his friend, and Hillary waited inside the hallway and greeted the Pullmans with open arms.

Fay asked where Tobias was when a familiar English voice sounded, “I am here, FP!”

Fay's face lit up. "Can I go and play racing?"

Helen smiled. "Yes, Tobias. Remember, she is only ten! No shooters!"

"Helen, it's Mungo's Track" Tobias laughed.

"Okay, I'll send a juice up!" Helen said. "He's like a big brother to her, but game consoles…"

"It's perfect!" Miles cut in, taking the Pullmans' coats, and hanging them onto a metal coat hanger. "Business to discuss. We shall leave you ladies to talk weddings!" Miles grinned, placing his arm around Jake.

Walking into Hillary's office, Jake placed himself onto the red fabric sofa. Suffocating the designer seat with his height, Jake relaxed, gripping a tumbler of whiskey.

Miles positioned himself at Hillary's desk. "Well, we are hitting stage three!" he placed his whiskey onto a marble coaster.

"The cash?" Jake asked.

"I cannot divulge at the amount, but Freidman can!" Miles winked.

"I have news," Jake commented. "The Turris Building is finally getting an interior makeover."

"So, we're on target!"

"Yes. W & J Pullman Law will be in operation next March."

"Staff?" Miles grinned.

"You of course, my silent partner. Working from London, if required!" Jake shook his head in disbelief. "I snatched Andrew Mason-Edwards and Patrick Jones-Gustav from Burrows & Burrows, Stanley Christopher-Black and Marc Aquilian from Battie and Thomas."

"You an attorney or a football team?" Miles whistled.

"How's the London office?"

"Small, but sufficient!"

Jake laughed. "Small, twelve floors and a restaurant, including a gym."

"It's no Philadelphia!" Miles answered back.

"The headquarters holds primary position,"

"I'm semi-retiring. The courtroom is in my past."

"That's what they all say." Jake swirled his glass. "I wonder why Freidman never picked up that you were in criminal law?"

"More criminal than law," Miles laughed.

"He'll be gone soon…." Jake grinned, walking over to Miles's desk and clinked glasses. "Cheers. To new beginnings!"

****

Montrose Gatehouse III - Mayfair - London

7th August 2006 - 6.00 p.m.

Hillary and Helen prepared evening meal. Helen sliced cucumber and tomatoes while Hillary steam-fried the small chicken pieces. Leaning into the white gloss island, holding a generous glass of white wine, she broke the silence.

"So, what's going on with Alice these days?" Hillary asked.

Helen put down her knife and grabbed her glass of white. "Gaining weight, shutting herself away from the public."

"I read about all the African projects and funding with the studio stuff!"

"Yeah, she's ploughed millions into the projects. After Fay died, I feel that Alice died too."

Hillary muttered, "Romano?"

"Loves her to death," Helen sighed.

"I never thought she would give up her music," Hillary said.

"After Fay, that was it." Helen continued to chop the salad and tossed it into a glass bowl. Suddenly stopping, Helen grinned. "When are you two going to marry!"

Miles's voice interrupted. "Tonight, if she'll have me!"

"Is that a proposal?" laughed Jake, standing behind his huge friend.

"Hillary Jonah, will you marry me?" he smiled, leaning on the island.

Hillary blushed. "I thought you were never going to ask!"

Miles sauntered around the island and pulled Hillary towards him. Placing his full moist lips upon hers, he kissed her passionately. Pulling away, he grinned. "I'll take that as a yes!"

Jake laughed, gripping Helen in his arms. "That's another wedding to pencil in!"

****

Arc Hopes Hospital - New Jersey

10th August 2006 - 3.00 p.m.

A magnetic field and computer-generated radio waves created detailed images of Allison's brain. Maxi gasped, wearing his white doctor's jacket. "Acute brain haemorrhages!"

Davis looked concerned. "How many?"

"Not sure!" he said, zooming into the scan. "Can you take it at another angle?" Maxi spoke to the technician.

"No wonder she's ill. The pain must be excruciating!" Davis responded, pushing his spectacles further up his nose brim.

Allison remained still, listening to the knocking, whirling, and grinding. Imprisoned within a tube, she looked at the hockey mask encasing her. A speaker sounded, with a male voice giving instructions. Not understanding any of it, she sighed. The platform she laid on moved forward.

Waiting by her side with a wheelchair were Maxi and Davis. A technician removed the equipment from Allison's head and slowly pulled her up into a sitting position.

"In the chair," commanded Davis.

"I have to change?" Allison answered.

"Not yet," Maxi beamed.

Allison knew something was wrong. "Okay, guys tell me!"

Maxi immediately pushed her away from the machine and out into the corridor. He wheeled her towards an elevator and pressed a button. Remaining silent, he continued to move her into the elevator until it reached room number three. Pushing the exhausted superstar into his consulting room, Maxi placed her next to his desk.

"Did it go well?" Romano appeared, standing next to his wife.

"Yes, with a complication." he said, staring at the superstar and her shocked husband.

Maxi then joined the conversation. "Alice, you are in surgery today!"

Allison spaced out while she gripped Romano's hand tight. "So, it's not menopause?" Romano said.

"That's my weight gain." Allison jumped in.

"That too," Davis responded. "Mostly your brain is haemorrhaging."

"Brain?" cried out Romano, nearly falling off his seat.

"I'm just giving you the facts. Alice has endured these symptoms for months. We cannot afford to let this bleed continue."

Allison interrupted. "Vomiting, headaches?"

"Intracranial haemorrhage, head trauma."

"Jake! Stella!" Allison and Romano said.

Maxi observed the couple. "You have had a few head injuries in the past and it could be anything causing the bleed."

"Well, it wasn't in the future," Allison replied.

Davis stepped in. "Look, we have to decompress her brain." He held his hand up. "Let me continue, releasing pooled blood will release pressure. Decompression is done through a burr hole procedure."

Romano's eyes lit up. "No way. Alice is not having a hole in her head!"

Maxi jumped in. "Romano, stop! Alice requires this operation, or she will die!"

"Die," Allison whispered.

"I know an excellent neurosurgeon. His name is Professor Oliver Striden. Romano, please!"

“I can sign,” Allison said, pulling her hand away from Romano.

“Alice!” Romano glared.

Pointing her forefinger at him. “We’ve already shared weddings together, do you want a funeral?”

“Okay, do it.” Romano accepted a tissue from Maxi to dry his eyes.

Allison signed her permission document and a purple-clad nurse pushed Allison into a preparation room.

Having bathed and put into a clean gown, Allison laid on a bed. The young blonde-haired nurse monitored her blood pressure and temperature, explaining that a sedative was going to be administered a few hours before the operation.

“Could I speak with my husband, please?” Allison enquired.

A middle-aged doctor walked into the room carrying a clipboard. He had dark brown cropped hair and a Balbo beard.

“Wow! I’m dead!” she said.

“Mrs Mancini, my name is Professor Striden. An honour to be in your presence.” He announced and took a seat next to her bed.

“Don’t tell me you’re a Templeton fan!” she muttered looking intensely at the handsome doctor.

“*Heavenly Body* is so catchy.”

“Pretty catchy for a song I scored at fifteen.”

“So, the operation...” He moved on from the polite chatter. “Doctors Jennings and Spink have explained the procedure.”

“I’m worried about my husband!”

“He’ll be fine. Once the janitor gets the mop,” he smiled. “We are going to sedate you. You will feel groggy for the next two hours, like someone spiked your drink.”

“Handsome man like you can spike my drink anytime!”

Oliver Striden laughed. “Alice, can I call you Alice?” Allison nodded. “You are the most beautiful woman

I have ever seen, and I won’t let anything happen to you.”

“Was the most beautiful woman,” Allison whispered. “In fact, a fat, menopausal woman who was once beautiful.”

Professor Striden disappeared from the room. Allison softly said “It’s my hormones that is why I’m window-shopping younger men! My God! Belinda window shops, not me! It’s the brain damage!”

A pleasant nurse walked into the bright, clinical room carrying a kidney bowl and a syringe. Inserting a canular earlier into Allison’s hand had made it easy for the nurse to insert the syringe into the plastic tube. Within twenty minutes, Allison became groggy.

Romano, dressed in his figure-hugging black jeans, strolled into the prep room. Witnessing Allison half-asleep, he immediately sat beside her, stroking her hand. "My love, please come through this. I can't live without you."

Allison mumbled with her eyes closed, "Romano, please stop being dramatic."

****

Arc Hopes Hospital - New Jersey

11th August 2006 - 1.00 a.m.

Romano anticipated Allison's arrival from the operating theatre. Sitting in the exquisite family room, Micky Connelly and Tomas Meier drank coffee from a cafetiere. Romano listened to the running water from the koi pond, it symbolised peace and tranquillity.

Romano's mobile rang. "Seb, what did I tell you? She's fine." Continuing his conversation with his son, he laughed and hung up. "Kids! I have two on honeymoon, one in London, one in LA, and the other in France. They are all over the place and still they pester me."

Tomas looked at Romano. "You haven't told them?"

Romano replied, "No, I don't want to worry them! Seb just called to see if the MRI went okay. I can't tell him she's having an operation."

Tomas smiled. "You'll have to tell them soon!"

"I know, I know." Romano held his hand up.

****

Arc Hopes Hospital - New Jersey

11th August 2006 - 7.00 a.m.

A fragile, pale finger stroked Romano's tanned hand. Slouched forward with his head embedded into the mattress, Romano sat up and grumbled, "Alice!"

Grinning, Allison muttered "Romano, my love?"

Romano activated the alarm. Within minutes, two nurses ran into the room.

"She's awake!" he announced with tears in his eyes. Davis and Maxi paced into the suite, reaching for their equipment. Shining an examination torch into Alice's eyes and checking the monitors, Davis smiled at Romano. "Your wife is here to stay! The operation was a success."

"She will be groggy from the operation, but recovery will be quick," Maxi said.

Romano burst into tears.

Maxi observed the scene. "Romano, you have not slept in your bed."

"I couldn't leave her!"

Davis tapped him on his shoulder. "Go take a shower and get some sleep."

"I…."

"Alice will be fine. Maxi and I must conduct more tests. Go!" Davis ordered.

Kissing his love, Romano dispersed from the room and organised new security to protect Allison. Micky, Tomas and himself headed back to Mancini Mansion for a well-deserved shower.

****

Mancini Mansion - New Jersey

11th - August 2006 - 9.30 a.m.

Romano stepped out of the steaming shower, refreshed. Rubbing his silver cropped hair, he felt lost. A knock interrupted his thinking. “Come in,” he shouted.

“My dear man, are you alright?” Sebastian asked, taking his seat in a wicker chair.

Walking into the bedroom with a towel around his waist, Romano sighed. Dropping himself onto the four-poster, he tugged another towel around his shoulders. “I thought it was just menopause?”

“Alice’s symptoms were aggressive at times,” Sebastian replied.

“It’s a success!”

“The operation?” Sebastian queried.

“She’s awake,” he said, moving from the bed and walking over into his dressing room. Romano heard Sebastian mumbling to someone. Popping his head around the doorframe, he stared.

Ella-Louisa and Dickie were speaking to Sebastian. Rising her head, she closed her eyes. "Dad! Get dressed!" she instructed.

Romano had paced out of his dressing room, naked. Sebastian grinned in delight at the size of his manhood, while Dickie averted his eyes.

"Ella, Dickie, you are supposed to be on your honeymoon!" Romano grinned.

"Dad, I am not discussing anything until you're wearing pants," she said.

Romano surrendered and sauntered back into the dressing room.

Sebastian could see why Allison had achieved five children with him. Becoming hot under his collar, Sebastian thought it would be a good time to remove himself.

Walking down the grand staircase, gripping his cane, Sebastian encountered the Mancini children. "Nathaniel, darling, your honeymoon?"

Nat winked and held Angel close. "We can continue our vacation later."

Sebastian Jr stepped in. "Mom?"

"Awake."

"Can we see her?" Benedict asked, closing the entrance door.

"Yes. Yes, and yes." Sebastian beamed at the questions being fired at him as he reached the bottom step.

Viewing the window, Sebastian could see Mercedes, BMWs, Ferraris, and a Maserati parked in parallel on the gravel driveway, while bodyguards paraded around the vehicles, chatting, and joking.

"How did you know about your mother?" Sebastian asked Rupert, still watching the activity outside.

Standing behind the fashionable man, Rupert replied, "Oliver and Maxi. Rachel can't fly now, so I alerted everyone. Here we are."

Turning around, Sebastian looked shocked. "You left her alone!"

"No, her dad is staying with her."

"Kenneth is a good man," sighed Sebastian with relief.

"You don't think I would leave my pregnant wife?"

"Darling, nothing surprises me these days." snarled Sebastian.

"Dad!" everyone shouted, glaring up Romano.

"Kids!" he shouted back.

Ella-Louisa and Dickie remained inside the master bedroom, packing her mother's night clothes and washbag. Simpson and his staff remained downstairs until Ella had completed her task.

Romano cried has he hugged his children in the marbled foyer. "She is going to be alright."

Ella-Louisa shouted from the master bedroom, "Dad, where is your bag?"

Romano stopped sniffling and looked up with his sons. "My God, she's louder than Alice!"

****

Arc Hopes Hospital - New Jersey

11th August 2006 - 1.00 p.m.

Allison sat up in bed dressed in her red satin pajamas and a blood stained bandaged wrapped around her head. The floral peach hospital suite invited the Mancini brothers to take their places on four suede sofas. Eating bananas and grapes, the brothers chatted between themselves, while Romano remained seated next to Allison in his relaxer chair. Ella-Louisa occupied the other side of the bed tutting at her brothers snacking on fruit.

Dickie, Sarah-Jane, and Angel had wandered into the fabulous koi gardens for a breath of fresh air. Chatting about their weddings and the news regarding their mother-in-law's operation.

Resting against her pillows, Allison restricted a smile due to the pain. She observed her family sitting around her. Ella-Louisa controlled the entire area. "You guys be quiet for Mom!" she hissed across the room.

Romano held Allison's hand. "She has your singing voice," he indicated towards Ella.

****

Mancini Mansion - New Jersey

11th August 2006 - 7.30 p.m.

Sarah-Jane Templeton-Mancini groaned, "Oh my God!"

"Sarah, whatever is the matter?" Sebastian asked from the bathroom.

Looking sidewards into a brass-plated dress mirror, she said, "I'm putting on weight!"

"No, you don't eat enough!" Sebastian shouted, looking at the razor cut bleeding on the side of his face. "Damn!" he huffed. Tearing a piece of tissue, he stuck it over his cut. "I hate shaving twice a day."

"I am. I have a tummy!" winced Sarah.

Rinsing his razor in the cloudy water, Sebastian dabbed his face with a blue hand towel.

"Okay, let me see!" He walked out of the bathroom.

Sarah-Jane, wearing a black lace thong and bra set, said, "Look!"

Sebastian glanced at the mirror wearing a grey towel wrapped around his hips, and whispered over Sarah-Jane's shoulder, "You have a tummy!"

“Thanks!” she huffed. “You weren’t supposed to say that!”

Sebastian shrugged. “What did I say?”

“Let me check something.” Sarah-Jane ran into the bathroom and opened the glass cabinet. Pulling out a long pink box, she shouted, “I won’t be long!”

Sebastian shook his head in despair. “Women!”

The bedroom around him reflected the artificial yellows and oranges from the bedside lights as shadows created silhouettes of the couple’s modern furniture. The king-sized bed displayed evidence of the couple’s lovemaking and Sebastian sat amongst the scattered bed sheets.

“Come in!” shouted Sarah-Jane, interrupting his reverie. Sebastian removed himself from the untidy bed and walked into the bathroom. Holding a pregnancy test up towards his face, she said, “Hello, Daddy!”

Sebastian, dumbfounded, muttered, “You are pregnant?”

“Yep, that’s why I am fat!” she laughed.

“How many weeks?” Sebastian glared at the test in Sarah’s hand.

“I don’t know! My mum gave me one of these!” Sarah said, opening the cabinet again.

“What’s Belinda giving you now?”

“Never mind that, let me pee!” Sarah shoved Sebastian out of the bathroom.

"A doctor will do the examination!" he said through the door.

Sarah-Jane held out the new test. "Two minutes!"

Sebastian and Sarah sat on the bed, smirking, leaning into one another. "Six weeks!" Sarah said. "I'm six weeks pregnant!" Stopping her excitement, she looked at Sebastian. "I am showing now?"

Sebastian dived off the bed and grabbed his laptop. Dialing into the connection, he looked on the Internet and his face grew into a wide smile.

"What? What? Tell me!" Sarah pulled at his naked arm.

"Twins. Triplets!"

"Three of you. Perfect!" she said, kissing him on the lips. Within minutes, Sarah's thong hit the carpet.

A knock at the door interrupted the couple. Sebastian yelled, "What?"

"Telephone," Simpson replied through the door.

"Important?"

"Important enough to make a phone call, sir."

"What time is it?" Sebastian giggled, playing with his wife's breasts.

"21:30."

Sarah grinned. "We missed dinner!"

"We live on the fruits of love!" Sebastian smirked.

"Tell them I'll ring back in the morning!" Sebastian replied, climbing on top of Sarah.

"Yes, sir!" Simpson responded, walking off.

"Where were we?" Sebastian was abruptly interrupted by Sarah's kiss.

****

Mancini Mansion - New Jersey

12th August 2006 - 7.00 a.m.

Sebastian and Oliver Dupont sat in silence within the stunning vintage dining room. The polished details and fine craftmanship of walnut elevated the style of Allison Templeton-Mancini.

Romano sat in the centre of the thirty-seater table, reading a leather-bound file that Sebastian had handed over. Bentley St Lavigne and Hardy Thompson-Jones remained seated next to Oliver.

Simpson and his staff carried trays of hot beverages into the room and collected six breakfast orders.

"I am so happy to conduct this meeting with you, Romano," coughed Sebastian, adjusting his pink cravat.

Romano looked up from his file and grinned. "Yep, just waiting for the kids!"

"I did telephone last night!" Hardy replied.

"Good thing Rup got the message!" Romano scoffed.

"Who, me?" Rupert emerged with Benedict. "We have notified the guys of our emergency family meeting." Benedict followed his brother, yawning.

Ella-Louisa strolled into the room wearing lilac pyjamas, coordinating robe, and fluffy unicorn slippers. Sebastian peered up from his reading. "Ella, darling, you ought to have dressed for this meeting."

Ella mumbled sleepily, struggling with her chair. "I am dressed!"

Sebastian shrugged and continued to read while Sebastian Jr. and Nathaniel sprang into the gathering, refreshed, and overjoyed.

"Morning, family," Nathaniel beamed.

Romano put down his file and looked at his son. "Your batteries charged?"

Both sons replied, "To the brim, father."

Following the Mancini breakfast orders, Sebastian Dupont commenced the family meeting.

"Your mother experienced surgery two days ago. There were no complications. She requires time to recover," Sebastian coughed again as he continued. "Your father is here to support your mother and..."

Jake Pullman and two legal representatives walked into the room. "Sorry, Sebastian, for our delay." Jake smiled and took his chair with his colleagues next to the Mancini children. Pulling out five files, Jake passed each one to the siblings.

"I shall continue!" said Sebastian.

Nathaniel jumped in, "Dad's going to die!"

Romano glared at Nathaniel. "So will you if you don't quiet down."

"Lawyers?" Nathaniel leaning in, staring towards Jake.

Oliver stated, "We are only going through issues if something does happen to your parents."

Dabbing her red watering eyes, Ella sniffled. "You don't think mom will recover from the brain haemorrhage!"

Oliver Dupont muttered, "What did I say, Ella? Your mom is recovering. She'll be fine."

Sebastian jumped in, "Let's continue. I must stress, if your parents do pass, then it is my job to overlook the entire estate."

Benedict looked confused. "I thought you were retired, Uncle Sebastian."

"And I thought you were going to be quiet," he glared. "The business's charities of your mother's will be overlooked by W & J Pullman Law. Mancini house will be run by Sebastian and Sarah-Jane."

"Wait," Sebastian Jr stepped in. "We live in London and at the Palmer Building in New York. We are only here to support dad!"

"That will change. Your mother requires you to take over, you are the first born. Your brothers and sister can stay or live in the property with you."

Sebastian glanced at Sebastian Jr. "Understand?"

Nodding, he had to tell Sarah-Jane that she would be permanently living at Mancini Mansion.

"Money. Your father's and mother's combined forty billion dollars will be controlled by W & J Pullman Law. Hardy and Bentley will manage the studios with the elective directors."

"What about you and Oliver?" Rupert said.

"I hope that my new neighbours will call upon us for afternoon tea." Sebastian smiled. "Don't worry. I will keep tabs on you."

"What about the rest of the Miller family?" sniffed Ella.

"What about them?" Oliver jumped in.

"Do they get anything?" Ella replied.

"No. They have their own wealth!" Sebastian said, closing the file. "We have finished!"

The five Mancini children looked at each other. "Can we have tea and discuss things with our partners?" Ella-Louisa muttered.

Oliver immediately stood up and paced to the door. "Breakfast will be served shortly. I will order tea, eight coffees, and a hot chocolate. Staff will take it into the conservatory."

"Thank you," Ella said, blowing her nose into a clean tissue.

When the siblings dispersed into the conservatory, Davis and Maxi walked into the prestige dining room. "That went well. I have ordered refreshments."

"Thank you. Will Simpson bring the tea in here?" Sebastian answered, leaning back against his high back chair.

Davis nodded, taking his seat across from Jake Pullman. "Don't blame yourself for this, Jake!"

"I caused her first head trauma. I did this."

"Accidents happen," Romano said, agreeing with Davis.

"She's much improved this morning. Ordered breakfast, double eggs…" Davis grinned at Romano.

"Double eggs," Romano whispered.

Davis continued, "Another couple of days and she will be eating eggs in Mancini Mansion."

"Romano!" Oliver blurted. "Looks like your Miss Loudmouth will be taking the reins again!"

Simpson walked into the dining room with a silver tray of refined beverages. Following him were two female staff. Oliver thanked the ladies as they dispersed.

Davis grabbed a cafetiere and china mug and poured coffee. “More news. Seb and Sarah-Jane are pregnant! Six weeks. Twins!”

Oliver Dupont lowered his mug onto a brown place mat. “Oh my God! When did you examine her?”

“This morning! Seb asked me to examine Sarah when he realised, I was attending the meeting. An appointment for them to proceed with a full ultrasound at my clinic is tomorrow at 11:00.”

Jake jumped in. “How do you know it is twins?”

“It’s either twins or a fetus with four arms,” Davis answered.

Romano stared at the conversation in awe. “I’m going to be a grandfather!” He cleared his throat. “Again!”

CHAPTER 13

Mancini Mansion - New Jersey

15th October 2006 - 9.00 a.m.

Steam swirled into every corner of the double bathroom. Laying in the Victorian free-standing bath, Romano Mancini grinned.

Allison poured soapy water over Romano's silver hair, groaning in delight as the warm, tantalising water ran over his olive skin. Sitting behind him, she whispered, "I won't surprise you next time!"

Removing himself from the tub, he placed a maroon towel around his manly hips. "I'll get back in soon, baby," he said, stroking Allison's cheek.

Stretching fully out, submerging in the lavender soap suds, Allison moaned.

Gelling his long-wet hair back and tying into a small ponytail, created the image that would stay with him until he died. Clipping away his stubble, he rubbed shaving foam onto his face. Staring at himself in the mirror, he whispered, "This fifty-six-year-old is looking like a ninety-six-year-old."

Allison laughed. "You look forty!"

Combing the razor over the foam, he began to see the fifty-six-year-old appearing again. Patting his face with a coordinating hand towel, he sprayed designer deodorant under his arms and plucked his eyebrows.

Climbing out of the bath, Allison grabbed a towel and followed her husband. Romano turned around and glared at his soaked wife. "Don't climb out of the tub by yourself! I'm here to help you."

"I can do it," Allison answered back.

"You might fall next time," Romano pleaded.

Dropping her towel, she whispered. "Come and get it!" Screeching, she ran over to the bed and dived naked onto the satin maroon duvet. Romano bounced on top of her smothering her in kisses.

Making love for an hour exhausted Allison. Romano removed himself from his panting wife and walked into his dressing room. Whistling while he selected a pair of his favourite black jeans and his typical dress shirt, he opted for underwear. Usually, Romano preferred not to wear under garments. The bodycon jeans clung to his muscular figure.

Selecting a pair of slip-on loafers, he looked at himself in the mirror. "Look good, my man. Looking good."

"Who are you talking to?" Allison said, splayed across the four-poster bed in her black lace underwear.

"Just gargling," Romano said, flexing.

Allison laughed. "I'm starving, I must dress." Forcing herself up from the bed, Allison shuffled into her dressing room and pulled a dress from the first available hanger. Squeezing herself into the garment, she was ready.

Opening the master bedroom door, Romano and Allison stepped into the hallway. A maid gasped. Romano put a finger over his mouth and asked for a full fried breakfast: fruit and cereal with black coffee and Earl Grey."

"Earl Grey, is that the classic tea, sir?" She bowed.

"Yes, what time is it?" He zipped up his fly.

The maid looked shocked and replied, "11:00, sir."

"Morning or night?" Allison giggled.

Continuing their walk towards the smaller dining room, Romano could hear chatter and laughing. "Our children. They don't know that you are home!"

The twelve-seater walnut round table displayed a selection of jams and pastries. Cafetieres, mugs, teacups, flamboyant cutlery, and napkins.

Ella-Louisa, Dickie, Oliver, Sarah Jane and both Sebastians, munched on their morning brunch, conversing and giggling.

"Good morning!" said Romano, stepping into the dining room.

Sebastian dropped his knife staining the white linen tablecloth. "Romano! How's Allison?"

"Dad! Mom!" Sebastian Jr and Ella jumped up and ran over to their parents. "You missed breakfast…we thought mom was still in the hospital!" Ella said, hugging both her parents.

"Good song," Allison added.

"We ordered breakfast." Romano smiled, looking at Allison bemused by her comment.

"Mom, your hair!" Sebastian and Ella simultaneously said, looking impressed.

"Do you like it? It's a bob cut," Allison laughed, releasing herself from her children.

"Bob? Don't tell us you're having another child." Oliver stood up and walked over to Romano, holding out his hand. "Respect, my man."

Romano shook his hand and replied, "Respect!"

Sebastian glared at Oliver. "What is that kind of talk?"

"English, Sebastian."

Romano took his place next to Ella-Louisa. "We celebrated yesterday. Alice got the all-clear."

Allison beamed. "So, I treated myself to a new cut. A new me!"

Simpson and his staff carried in a selection of cereals and fruits on silver platters. "Your coffee, sir."

"You're a gentleman and a scholar, Simpson." Romano said.

"I am whatever your needs require."

"All we require is a second course."

Ella looked at her dad's bowl filled to the brim with fruit. "Second course?"

"I have two months of eating to catch up on," Romano smiled, pouring his coffee.

Sebastian and Oliver shrugged, bewildered.

Allison continued to devour her fruit and buttered toast.

Romano spoke while he continued to eat his muesli. "Your mom and I have decided that it is important that our children live here with us."

Dickie and Ella-Louisa looked at one another. "That's impossible."

"Six months here, six months in your English castle!" Romano said, tucking into a bowl of grapefruit.

Oliver Dupont sniggered into his napkin. Dickie said, "My work is in London."

"Banking?" Romano jumped in. "Do it in New York!"

"My role is in London," Dickie replied.

"Sebastian will sort out a split role, six months in London, six months in New York, he's got contacts."

Sebastian choked on his Earl Grey. "You ever need someone to balance your books, Romano's a good cook," Oliver laughed.

"Seb, you, and Sarah-Jane will take over the house when we die." Romano pointed his knife towards the couple. "But you will live here now! I'm in talks with Sam Styliani regarding the nursery. Sarah-Jane, design to your heart's content!"

"It's sad that Julia is dead. Sam will do a great job!

Let me help!" Allison jumped in.

Sebastian and Sarah-Jane looked confused at one another. "How did you know that I'm pregnant?"

"Vedic astrology," Romano laughed, buttering a bread roll. "Also, Davis told us."

"Rup," Ella said.

"He too will live here. The house in LA will be a workhouse, like dad and I used to have." Allison beamed.

Romano continued, "Nat, the same. Ben is different with his tennis tournaments, but he will reside here with Leon!"

"Dad, how do you know Nat and Ben will move here?" Ella asked.

"They asked," Allison grinned.

"These are your mother's wishes." Romano rang the bell for his fried breakfast. Gripping his mug, he said, "Your mom is with me all the way. We talk regular, don't we, baby?"

Allison gripped Romano's hand. "Every night. Babies in the house will bring it back to life. I kind of missed out on you guys, with my music and film career."

Oliver Dupont placed his fork down onto his plate. "It's good to have you back, Alice."

Mancini Mansion - New Jersey

15th October - 2006 - 12.30 p.m.

The cool autumn breeze danced across the fern green golf course. Romano Mancini and sixty-one-year-old Craig Welling controlled their designer trolly bags with their remote controls. "I can believe you are growing your hair. We were all concerned you were going to flip over Alice." Craig said, adjusting his red tartan flat cap.

"I nearly did," Romano answered, walking forward. "Alice stopped me."

"Why?"

"I knew something was wrong. She had visited Maxi's clinic after she was ill. She complained about headaches, vomiting, hot flashes, mood swings. At Nat's and Ella's wedding, she crumbled. Menopause. Broke down. I organised an MRI with Davis. Good thing I did. I had to be strong."

Stopping by Romano's side, Craig answered, "Why MRI?"

"The headaches!"

"Alice could have died," Craig looked down at the grass.

"I'm lucky," Romano sighed, leaning against his bag.

"She's a new woman!" Craig said.

"I can't keep up with her in bed. Her hormones are killing me," Romano winked.

"I always knew you were nuts," Craig replied.

****

Inside the five-bedroom house, Adele was in deep conversation with Lucinda and Max La-Mount-Martinez. Max and Lucinda sat on the brown leather corner sofa, drinking red wine, while Adele chopped potatoes and onions in her pine wood open-plan kitchen. Reaching for the pepper mill, she noticed a figure sat elegantly at the island. "Alice, when did you arrive?" Adele said, jumping out of her skin.

Allison laughed. "I did knock, but you were all gossiping, and I got discharged a few days ago."

Adele offered Allison a glass of red merlot. Lucinda jumped up and ran over to hug her friend. In response, Allison waved at Max. "So, spill the beans, what's been going off?"

Lucinda blushed. "You look great, Alice. I could do with what you're on!"

"Estrogen?" Allison took a sip of her wine, screwing her pretty features in confusion.

Adele put her knife down onto the chopping board. "When you were in hospital, Lucinda, Max, Craig, and I visited. Who did not visit you?"

Allison looked to either side of them and thought. "Belinda and Donny! She's in LA for work."

"That's what she wanted you to think," Lucinda said, grabbing a stool.

"What?" Allison said.

"It's called lying, Alice." Max jumped in from the sitting area. "Deception, not telling the truth…"

Allison looked up at the ceiling. "What's she done now?"

"She left Donny!" Lucinda blurted.

"She what?" Allison spat out her wine.

"She's living in London!" Adele said, wiping Alice's face.

Allison spat out her wine again. "With Charles Medley-Garrett?"

"Try to get some in your mouth," Max said.

"He's seven years younger than her! How long has this been going on?"

"Since Rup's wedding. She sneaked off with him earlier that evening. The lovebirds made a nest in one of your bedrooms," Max voiced, pouring himself another glass of wine. "Then he re-joined the wedding party and danced with you.

Allison drank the rest of her wine just to spit it out again.

Lucinda looked concerned. “Are you feeling okay, Alice?”

Adele grabbed Allison’s hand. “We didn’t want to upset you, with your woman issues.”

“Brain damage is not a ‘woman issue!’”

“Could have fooled me,” Max said.

“I got the all-clear yesterday,” Allison added.

Lucinda and Adele squealed in delight and threw another hug at her.

“You’re the best, Alice.” Max gave a thumbs up.

“Thanks, guys. Tell me more. What about Donny?”

“He’s relieved. She’s been driving him mad. He’s filing for divorce!” Lucinda announced.

“Sarah-Jane didn’t say anything.”

“She will not have anything to do with Belinda.” Adele continued to prepare lunch.

Grabbing a carrot, Lucinda went on, “Angel is okay with it. Both Sarah-Jane and Angel are still speaking.”

“Sarah-Jane’s tolerance for her mother is identical to Donny’s: zero. Belinda can be too much. I noticed at the wedding she was checking out men, even my bodyguard.”

“I believe she’s pregnant,” Adele whispered into the chopping board.

The room hit a rock-solid silence. Allison whispered, "Fifty-two-year-old Charles's baby?"

"She is besotted by Charles and has quit the soap series in LA. She has moved in with him," grabbing a stool beside his wife, Max continued. "She was screwing him at Harlsby-Hall. Everyone thought the next morning she had a hangover, but it was morning sickness."

"I forgot to mention, Andrew married Penelope Tomkinson-Clifton in September. Family only, but it was beautiful. She is working in the *Galleria* for David." Lucinda noted.

"And I thought I had brain damage!" Allison blurted.

"She is good for Andrew."

"What about Belinda?"

"She cut herself off from us, but Donny is keeping the house in the Hamptons and suing her arse off for adultery."

"Jake's team?"

"Yes. Jake's office is in Philadelphia but doesn't open until March. He hired a small team in Manhattan, multi-million-dollar office block!" Adele pointed out, placing her meat loaf into the oven.

"I need to talk with him and Helen. I have not seen them since August."

"Alice, we kept this hidden because we didn't want to upset you. But Romano…" Max got interrupted.

"Romano knew?" Allison smiled at Max.

"He's really annoyed with her." Adele gripped her glass. "Not because of what she has done, but because she blamed you."

"What did I do?" Allison said.

Romano was standing directly behind her, cuddling her waist, and caressing her neck with kisses. Allison shuddered at his warm, sensuous breath massaging her skin.

"She, said that you had the affair with him, that you rejected him. Belinda was just a shoulder to cry on!" Lucinda jumped in.

Allison couldn't believe what she was hearing. "I danced with him once."

"Baby, I love you." Romano gripped her more tightly and continued to kiss her.

"There's more," Craig announced, walking up to the island and grabbing a beer. "Sarah-Jane may not be Donny's."

"We were friends for forty-five years," Allison said.

Lucinda looked at Allison. "Did we really know her? At the age of thirteen she'd sneak out of school and spend time in the boy's school dormitory at St Augustine's."

"Did she?" Allison said in shock. "Who do we think is Sarah-Jane's father?"

Romano cut in. "I don't want Alice upset."

Craig, Romano, and Max looked at one another. Grabbing their beers, the sound of metal lids hit the pine worktop. Downing his drink, Craig looked at Allison and said, "If I tell you, will you be, okay?"

Allison nodded. Romano stood next to her, supporting his wife with one arm around her. "Paul Freidman," Craig replied.

"Freidman?" Allison whispered in disarray.

"Behind Donny's back, Belinda spent most of her time at Freidman's house. Early days with the band and when Freidman was sacked." Craig said.

"So that explains why Belinda wasn't maternal with Sarah-Jane and Donny was," Lucinda said.

"My grandchildren will have Freidman's genes!" Allison screamed.

****

Mancini Mansion - New Jersey

15th October 2006 - 7.00 p.m.

Lounging at his desk, Romano Mancini held the handset to his ear. Relaxing in his leather high back chair he crossed his long legs on top of the desk.

"Micky? Yeah, it's me. We're going to LA on Wednesday. Not sure, 9:30 a.m. we are in the Hamptons. No, I don't have a car yet, that's why I'm asking you. Okay, bye."

Allison lounged on his black sofa, smiling. “I’m impressed you and Adele protected me from Belinda’s shenanigans.”

Romano gazed across at her. “I can’t afford for you to have a relapse.”

“Believe it or not Belinda did get on my nerves.”

“She always did yell a little too much.”

Ella-Louisa burst into the office and yelled, “Pizza!”

“Speaking of yelling…” Romano said.

CHAPTER 14

Santiago Del Porto - Bel-Air - Los Angeles

18th October 2006 - 2.00 a.m.

Rupert Templeton-Mancini stretched out face-down on top of the king-sized bed, snoring. Rachel shuffled around the dark bedroom holding the bottom of her back. The pain was becoming annoying, and she wondered if a hot bath would soothe her throbbing backache.

Shuffling into the bathroom, Rachel ran the hot water faucet. Sitting on the toilet seat, she felt a warm dampness seeping through her pyjama's bottoms. Looking down, she muttered. "My waters!"

Undressing, she had to take the pain away before she called for Rupert. Climbing into the deep, relaxing warm water of the double corner bath, she sighed. Laying back and meditating, it wasn't long before the pain faded. Relaxing, Rachel began to close her eyes.

Rupert walked into the bathroom to pee. Standing half-asleep, he didn't noticed Rachel in the bath. Flushing the toilet, he strolled to the double vanity unit and washed his hands. Looking down at the floor, he felt clothing with his bare foot. "What the hell?"

Waking up, he turned around and witnessed Rachel relaxing in the bath. "Sweetie, what are you doing at this time in the morning?"

With her eyes closed she mumbled “Backache. My waters broke!”

“What?” Rupert panicked.

“Slow down. I don’t need the stress,” she said. “This is lovely.”

“What do I do?” Rupert replied, bending down by the side of the bath.

“Put some pants on and call Doctor Grey. His number is in the kitchen.”

“Are we having the baby at home?”

“No, I’m having the baby at home.”

Rupert rushed into the bedroom and pulled on his jogging bottoms and his Templeton t-shirt. “Do you want some Earl Grey?”

“Shut up, Rup.”

“Be right back!” he said, rushing out of the bathroom and down the glass staircase. He glanced at the wall clock: 4:30 a.m. “How long has she been in the bath?” he muttered to himself, removing the kettle from the stove.

Rupert rang Doctor Grey and explained that Rachel’s waters had broken. Drinking his tea, he explained that she wasn’t pushing yet. The doctor agreed that he should be present to prepare for a home birth.

Rupert rang off and went back upstairs carrying his half cup of Earl Grey. When he walked into the bathroom, Rachel had run some more hot water. Pulling up a stool, Rupert sat against the tub and spoke. "Are you in pain?"

Rachel replied, "Not yet."

"Doctor Grey is on his way! Looks like it is a home birth, so he must prepare."

"Why?"

"Because you told me to ring him when the baby was coming." Rupert said taking a sip from his cup.

"Oh, Rup, you make a fantastic father!"

"Do you want me to bring you a t-shirt? It doesn't matter if it gets wet."

"Yes, please. Good idea. I know the doctor will see my…but I can cover up on top!"

Rupert ran into Rachel's dressing room and pulled out an *I Love New York* t-shirt dress. Taking it into the bathroom, Rupert commented, "I didn't know you liked New York."

"I got it in New Jersey."

Rupert helped Rachel pull on the shirt. "Do you feel better?"

"Now that you're here."

"Mom and dad would like us to live in Mancini Mansion and we can design one of the nurseries."

"I would love that. The schools are brilliant up there, and we would be near our family."

Rupert put his finger up. "Your dad can come. There's a gamekeeper's house on the grounds."

Water splashed. Rachel hugged Rupert with dripping wet arms. Rupert laughed. "I'll take that as a yes! We will keep this house for when I am filming in LA. Your dad can keep his and use it for a holiday home!"

"Perfect! When can I start designing?"

"When you have given birth to Miss Templeton-Mancini."

The security gate rang. One of the security guards buzzed in Doctor Grey. Parking his BMW next to Rupert's Zonda F Roadster, the doctor collected his medical bag and ran inside the luxury five-bedroom house.

Rupert greeted him by the interior entrance door. Explaining the outcome of the early morning, Doctor Grey prepared himself for the birth, setting up his sterilising equipment, laying plastic sheeting onto the floor and bed. Rupert had also selected a set of clean underwear, tampons, and pyjamas for Rachel. His daughter had a pink baby grow and diaper waiting for her.

At 6:00 a.m. Doctor Gey continued to monitor Rachel, still soaking in the bath. She heaved and a drop of blood surfaced to the top of the water. "I feel like going to the toilet."

"No toilet, Rachel. You are having contractions. Push!"

Rupert knelt on the tiled floor, holding Rachel's hand. She heaved again. Rupert was worried that the baby would drown in the water.

"Push, push, push, Rachel." Doctor Grey instructed. Suddenly he lifted out of the water a dark-haired baby girl. Doctor Grey cut the umbilical cord and wrapped her in a soft white towel, handing the baby over to Rupert.

Rupert gazed at his beautiful baby girl while she stared back quietly at her father.

"Am I okay to get out? I'm wrinkled." Rachel said exhausted.

Climbing out of the bath with the help of Doctor Grey, Rachel jumped into the shower and changed into her pajamas. With a towel tied around her head, she walked into the bedroom and witnessed Rupert feeding his daughter with a bottle of formula. Doctor Grey supervised the new father.

"She is already dressed!" Rachel said, surprised.

"Yes, he has put her diaper on. Have you a name?"

Rupert and Rachel announced, "Autumn-Marie."

****

Mancini Mansion - New Jersey

18h October 2006 - 8.30 a.m.

Standing in the marbled foyer of Mancini Mansion, Ella-Louisa gripped onto Dickie's hand. "Why do we have all this luggage packed, darling?" he spoke, gesturing towards a mound of designer baggage.

Ella glared at her handsome husband and replied, "Dickie, I don't know how long we are going to be staying in LA!"

Sebastian and his pregnant wife Sarah-Jane walked towards the marquis and marchioness.

"Did you pack?" Sarah asked Ella-Louisa, observing the mountain of bags stacked against the walnut table.

"She certainly did!" Dickie pointed over his shoulder.

Ella sighed, staring at the beautiful white roses placed in a crystal vase. "Mom's favourites!"

"The foyer will continue to display fresh roses until the day she dies!" Sebastian said.

"Dad did it from day one. The staff regularly change them as part of their duties." Ella smiled.

Simpson and two of his staff carried Sebastian's three huge suitcases.

"Can't be too sure how long the stay will be," Sarah said. Both Dickie and Sebastian looked up at the ceiling in despair.

Romano walked down the grand staircase wearing his new tight Sylvester-Montgomery jeans. Black dress shirt, black western boots, and a long black leather trench coat.

Romano's shoulder-length silver hair was tied back with a black leather tie.

"Okay, guys. Ready?" he said.

"Wow, dad. You look great!" both siblings said at the same time.

"I don't know about great, but I look like Romano Mancini!" he winked.

Allison strolled behind Romano, wearing a black fitted trouser suit and stilettos.

Ella-Louisa gasped. "Mom, you look beautiful!"

"I expect to look good all the time!" she laughed, caressing her bob cut. Wearing her typical piercing red lipstick against her pale complexion, she completed the style perfectly.

"Right, have a safe flight, and we will see you in LA tomorrow." Romano leaned in and kissed Ella on her cheek.

Climbing into the first limousine, Ella-Louisa, Dickie, Sebastian, and Sarah-Jane made themselves comfortable on the grey leather interior. Max-B-Turner, Melvin Davis-Grey, Mark Barker, and Micky Connelly chatted against a vacant silver limo parked behind the siblings. Simpson and his staff began loading vehicle number three, a black Range Rover.

The first limo manoeuvred across the gravelled driveway and disappeared. Following close behind was the black Range Rover. Clearing all security checks, the first and second vehicle signalled left and advanced towards the airport.

Mark Barker pulled down the privacy window and turned towards Ella-Louisa. "The drive is two hours. Is your sickness under control?"

Ella-Louisa stared at Mark while Dickie looked confused. "Sickness?"

"Yep, I'm pregnant!" she muttered, looking out of the tinted window.

"How many weeks?" Dickie asked, grabbing Ella into his arms.

"Five."

The car erupted into celebrations and Sarah-Jane hugged her sister-in-law with a beam.

****

Mara Casa - The Hamptons

18[h] October 2006 - 9.30 a.m.

The silver limo declined down an embankment towards a procession of antique houses situated against a glorious blue coastline. Opening the metal security gates, a uniformed guard gestured for the limo to enter. When the car parked outside the house, Allison stepped out of the rear passenger seat into the brilliant sunshine. Placing her shades over her eyes, Romano followed her.

"Donny," Romano smiled. "My man!"

Donny Davis strolled out of his spacious six-bedroom house wearing loose white linen trousers and an oversized linen shirt. Flip-flopping across the driveway towards his friends. "Romano. Alice," he said, falling into a huge hug.

"I didn't know you owned a Bentley," Allison giggled.

"I don't!"

Romano admiring the black Bentley Continental GT. "Whose is it?"

"Mine!" laughed Jake Pullman.

"Jake!" Allison ran across to him, crunching on the gravel. Helen was standing directly behind him. "Helen!"

"Calm down!" Romano shouted. "She'll have a relapse if she's not careful."

Walking inside Donny's home, Allison and Romano gazed around the cathedral-shaped foyer. Stepping into the open-plan sitting room, Allison whispered, "Wow!" at the mesmerising ocean view from the floor-to-ceiling windows.

"I don't understand why she has given all this up," Allison said to Romano.

Donny coughed. "A fool. I don't care about her."

Jake and Helen had taken their seats outside on the glass balcony that overlooked the crashing waves. Donny prepared hot beverages and joined the couple outside. Following behind were Romano and Allison, still admiring the views.

Taking her rattan seat while Romano pushed her against the glass table, Allison looked over at Donny. "Are you okay?"

"Happy, relaxed, and overjoyed," he replied, pouring tea into floral teacups.

Jake laughed. "Yes, he's keeping the house, car, and his fortune. Plus, compensation for distress."

Donny grinned. "Ten million dollars!"

Romano whistled, accepting his mug of coffee. Allison tapped Romano on his knee. "Don't worry, I won't sue you for distress!"

Helen broke out into laughter. "You and Romano split? You are joined at the hip!"

Donny continued to speak against the sound of crashing waves. "That English guy refused her advances on a few occasions. Apparently, he was fond of someone else." Donny sipped his coffee and looked towards the ocean. "She broke him down, like she does with everything.

Stupid woman!"

Allison glanced at Romano and remained silent. Jake stepped in. "How is Sarah-Jane?"

Donny laughed. "Big!"

"Twins! Do we know the sex?" Helen smiled.

"They want it to be a surprise." Romano said.

“Donny you will have to stay at Mancini Mansion when the twins are born.” Allison said, gripping Romano’s leg.

“You know, Alice, Belinda and you were never right together. Oil and water. She was jealous.”

Allison listened to Donny and agreed that she did at times feel used. “Lucinda is your true friend. I hope I’m still part of the clique.”

Standing up from her seat, Allison walked around the table and hugged Donny. “You’ll always be part of the clique.”

****

NYC International Airport - New York

19th October 2006 - 11.30 a.m.

Splashing cold water onto his refreshed face, Romano Mancini gasped for stability. Staring at his aging features in the private bathroom’s illuminated mirror, he paused. Standing right behind him was Allison, looking radiant in her favorite tweed clothing and bob cut. She winked fastening her blouse.

Strolling from the restroom, he walked over to the Mancini security who were sipping coffee and soft drinks. “Guys, breakfast is on me.” Romano fist-bumped each one.

“Cheers, boss!”

Opening the tinted glass private suite door, Romano whistled. “Alice, food!”

Sitting in the private suite of round glass tables and blue suede loungers, two attendants offered Allison and Romano a blue leather-bound menu.

“Pancakes, hashbrowns, bacon, egg on rye. Please.” Romano smiled, handing over his menu.

“Romano!” Allison scoffed. “I haven’t chosen yet.”

“I forgot, black coffee and another whiskey, please!” Romano ignored her moans.

Allison ordered her brunch. “I’m starved!” she beamed, holding her husband’s hand.

“That’s one way of keeping fit!” he said.

****

LA International Airport

18th October 2006 - 11.00 a.m.

Allison peered through the porthole window, watching the private 737 hit the runway. “My God, it’s already eleven!”

“We go back three hours.” Romano laughed. “Why people want to work in LA is beyond me.”

“You did!”

“Touche.”

“Can we have some fun later? It’s been a brainless week!”

“Brainless? Did our session at the airport, not satisfy you?”

“Yes, but I need more. Nothing makes sense. Belinda running away with a toy boy. She’s dead to me! Now, more new life coming into the world.”

“Rup’s baby is due any day,” Romano sounded excited.

“My hormones are raging today!” Allison sighed, staring at the tarmac.

“We’ll have sex later, calm you down,” Romano said.

The engines rumbled and the jet shuddered while the plane directed itself towards the asphalt. Romano continued eating his lemon cheesecake, scraping his plate clean. At the rear of the plane, two suited bodyguards chatted with the flight attendants.

Security boarded the famous Mancini jet while the flight attendants collected the family’s documents. Passing clearance, two SUVs were parked on the tarmac, while the family’s luggage got unloaded from the cargo hold.

Romano tapped his stomach in delight. Micky Connelly helped Romano to his feet and escorted him down the boarding stairs and into the first car. Tomas assisted Allison, following her overindulged husband.

The two SUVs maneuvered past vast of people. Camera flashes and fluttering message boards covered every available space. The sun rays beat down upon the crowds, while a warm breeze blew past the commotion.

In the back passenger seats, the Mancinis ducked their heads below the blacked-out windows as the vechicles accelerated away from the airport. Within twenty minutes, the cars were pulling into Porta Del Castello.

Security opened the electronic gates, and the motorcade followed the driveway up to the mansion's double doors. Nathaniel and Angel waved while anticipating their arrival. Six staff also accommodated themselves behind the excited couple.

The first car stopped. Micky Connelly stepped out with the driver. Nodding to Nathaniel, he opened the door. Romano stepped out, wearing his Sylvester-Montgomery shades. Opening his arms, he shouted "Son!"

"Dad!" yelled Nathaniel. "What happened to your hair?"

"What?"

"It's so long and white!"

Allison laughed "Silver."

"True. How are you doing, dad?" Nathaniel looked concerned, hugging him. "Mom!" He ran over to Allison. "Your hair!"

"A new me, it's called a bob cut."

"Dad! Mum!" Angel hugged Romano and Allison.

The second car approached. Mancini staff removed the couple's luggage. By now, Romano chatted with his old staff standing on the stone steps.

Nathaniel and Angel beamed. Allison looked at the cuddling couple. "What are you two up to?"

Everyone went silent. "We are pregnant!" Nathaniel put his arm around Angel's waist and beamed with pride.

"That is wonderful!" Allison screamed.

Romano and Allison hugged Angel and Nathaniel on the tiled steps. "When?" Allison blurted.

"June!" Angel smiled.

"Come inside, everyone!" Nathaniel called.

The staff unpacked the SUVs and showed the security men to their rooms. Ella, Dickie, and Mark were staying next door with Rupert, Rachel, and Autumn. Jono Murrey greeted the security men with fist-bumps, before they dispersed with the house staff.

Walking into Porta Del Castello brought happy memories back for Romano. He had purchased the property in 1973 when he was twenty-three. Allison had moved in with him in 1977. Romano smiled at the tiled staircase and the Greek pillars. He had fun chasing Allison around the foyer, especially naked. At that time, they didn't employ staff. 1980 is the time when the first set of staff came to live at Porta Del Castello and Romano had built ten small houses adjacent to the gate house.

Chattering and laughing brought him back down to earth. Walking into the immense sitting room, he took his place in a leather recliner. "We have more news!" Nathaniel smiled.

Romano looked around. Rupert and Rachel strolled in with a carrycot. "When?" he gasped in amazement.

Allison jumped up. "You have had her!"

Rupert said, "Yesterday morning at 7:00. Really, we shouldn't have brought her out yet. You know, inoculations! But we would have only had to do the same coming home from the hospital."

"You delivered her at home?" Allison stepped in.

"No choice," Rachel spoke, carrying Autumn over to her grandparents. "It was her time."

Romano investigated the carrycot and the beautiful little girl lay peacefully wearing a pink baby gown. Stroking her small soft hand, he began to cry. Allison cuddled Romano, gently cooing at the baby.

"Dad! Don't cry." Nathaniel bent down and looked at his father.

"She's beautiful, just like her grandmother."

Allison produced a beautiful smile and kissed Romano on the side of his cheek. "Do you have a name?"

“Autumn Marie Templeton-Mancini.” Rupert proclaimed.

“A new Mancini,” sniffled Romano.

****

Santiago Del Porto - 19th October 2006 - 7.00 p.m.

It was important for Romano and Allison to have family dinner all together on their first night. Rachel had joined the family for the meal but vacated after an hour because of exhaustion. Miss Templeton-Mancini was screaming for her milk. Romano couldn’t wait for Rupert’s family to move into Mancini Mansion.

Two large wooden tables stood next to the backlit pool. Sebastian, Sarah-Jane, Nathaniel, Angel, Rupert, Ella-Louisa, and Dickie were chatting over risotto. Romano and Allison observed their children’s closeness.

“We are lucky,” he whispered, cuddling Allison.

“I wish Benedict were here,” she sighed, clinching her glass of red wine.

Shadows cast along the ripples of water reflecting from the pool. Crickets sang against the clear starry sky.

Ella spoiled the tender moment when she announced, “I am pregnant!”

Romano and Allison pulled away from one another and stared at their daughter in surprise. “You’re what?”

“June!” Dickie grinned, holding Ella’s hand.

"June!" yelled Angel. "Me too!"

"Oh, my word," Allison whispered while Romano remained in shock.

"We must have...." Angel put her hand over Nathaniel's mouth.

"Two more. There will be five grandchildren." Romano blurted. "We need another table."

****

CHAPTER 15

Castrum Place - Rye - New York

1st November 2006 - 4.00 p.m.

The musty smell of decomposing leaves surrounded the body of a decapitated bodyguard. Paul Freidman paced into his Art Deco sitting room. "What do you mean my warehouses are closed?" he yelled into his mobile phone.

The seventy-year-old dropped onto a red velvet chaise lounge. "Where's my money?"

A deep cough interrupted his conversation. Miles Peterson stood behind Paul's lounger, wearing his black designer suit, long cashmere coat, and grey silk tie. "What's the matter, Freidman?" he grinned, taking a seat across from him. Crossing his huge legs, he struggled to maintain his position on Paul's dollhouse chair.

"What are you doing here?" Paul grunted, slamming his mobile closed.

"Heard you were having problems with your small business," Miles said. "Apparently, Europe is shut down."
"We don't need Europe."

"I need a drink!" Miles spat, walking towards Paul's bar. Pouring himself a whiskey he noticed a shadow behind him.

"What the hell!" Paul called out.

"Want some legal advice?" Jake Pullman said, crossing his arms. "I'll only charge you for a glass of whiskey."

"How did you get in?" Paul asked.

"Front door," Jake grinned, wearing his long black cashmere coat.

Paul looked out of the window searching for his bodyguard. "Why are you two here? You need money for child support?"

"Child support? It's the space age, Freidman. We have abortions now. And unless you want me to postnatally abort you, keep away from my wife," Jake said.

"Sit down!" Miles stepped in. "You know, you are the most egocentric man I have ever met!"

"What are you talking about?" spat Paul.

Miles laughed. "You want a drink, Jake?"

"Sure do. Make it a reserve!"

"Certainly," Miles smiled, leaning against the bar. "You know, I love smashing things." Miles picked up a crystal tumbler and dropped it onto the oak flooring. Brittle particles scattered everywhere. Miles crunched on a piece of glass while he opened a new bottle of reserve whiskey.

"That is worth more than your life!" Paul yelled.

"So, what, a buck fifty?" Jake laughed. "That's what Helen charges per hour for real estate."

"Helen? It was an accident. I wasn't thinking," Paul said.

“Was Eva Moulin?” Miles cut in.

“As bad at sex as she was with money. She had to go.” Paul emptied his glass and took his seat again on the chaise lounge.

“Go where?” Jake answered, accepting his glass from Miles.

“Same place everybody else does.” Paul glared at Miles raiding his drink bar.

“What about the hit and run?” Jake asked.

“What about it? Stupid fool walked in front of my car.”

“That stupid fool was Dennis Dayton, Helen’s father!” Jake replied.

“Accidents happen.” Paul shrugged.

“Never to you!” Miles piped up.

“Before I left New York, I would pay him a final visit. Had my driver follow him. Lucky for me, he stepped out into the road!” Paul glared at Miles.

“So, you told your driver to step on the gas!” Jake answered.

“No witness, no crime,” Paul smirked.

“You hit Dayton just like you attacked my wife,” Jake held out his glass for a refill.

“No. You wife asked for it.”

Paul remained silent and listened to the fire crackling. Miles's deep voice broke the silence. "I married Stella last week!"

Paul glared at him. "She's dead."

"That is what you think," another voice called from behind.

Turning around, Paul laughed. "Mel Dominic?"

"Good to see you, Paul. I'll have what you're having," said the Argentinian.

"I'm having a bad day," Freidman said.

"So was Stella," Mel smiled, crossing his legs, and accepting his drink from Miles. "But your Neanderthals got in the way."

"You killed them!" Paul said, eyes wide open.

"I love a good piece of meat!" Mel laughed.

"My bodyguard?"

"Couldn't even guard himself," he continued to laugh. "The best thing is that the police think you did it!"

"You framed me!"

"A stickleback trying to play against a shark," Mel laughed and snapped his jaws. "Taking my drug business was your first mistake. Killing my lover Eva was your last mistake!"

"You and Eva Moulin?" Paul said.

"She was a ballerina in Argentina. Beautiful. We used to make love under the stars! She broke my heart. I followed her all the way to New York and found her dealing with shit like you!"

"She was in love with me!" Paul cut in.

"That's what they always say, old man!" laughed Mel. "You had a kid with Stella. Good looking boy. Be a shame if something happened to him."

"What?" screamed Paul.

"Stella was pregnant when I rescued her. Miles always kept your side of the bed warm even on the days he wasn't contracted."

"The kids mine!" Miles jumped in.

Paul glared at Miles. "Is this true? You were only allowed to sleep with her on my say!"

Mel continued, "I love the gallery!"

"What gallery?

"What gallery?" Mel grinned, sipping his drink. "You have good taste in whiskey, Paul!" He raised his glass. "Jake, my man, go and have a browse in the room across the hallway."

Jake stood up and walked out into the hallway and headed for the door facing the sitting room. Stepping inside, he witnessed the most bizarre scene: candles burning in different directions, an abandoned fireside armchair placed in the middle of the floor, a side table with a box of white tissues and a metal bin. But it was the scene on the wall that unnerved him. Thousands and thousands of photographs of Helen. Helen with dark hair, Helen with blonde hair, Helen leaving the office, arriving at the office, Helen on holiday.

Jake sat down in the chair and stared at the wall of photographs. "I'll kill him."

"Pauls got it bad!" Mel said, smirking from the doorway.

"Always knew he was a jerk," Jake replied walking back into the sitting room.

Paul ran past Mel and pounced on the top of Jake. Suddenly a hand pulled Paul's head back, and a stainless steel hunting knife sliced its way across Paul's throat. Blood dripped from the clean-cut line. Falling onto the floor, burbling, trying to hold onto his throat, Paul Freidman's eyes bulged out of his head.

Continuing with their drinks, the two gentlemen ignored the mess. Jake stepped around the crimson pool and joined them.

"Don't you just love sliced meat?" Mel said.

"That wasn't kosher," Miles laughed.

Jake sat down and continued to enjoy his whiskey.

"So did you pay all the staff off?" a voice sounded from behind Jake.

"I did…" Miles said.

Jake turned around and was shocked to see Oliver Dupont standing like he had just come off a catwalk. “Right! Wire transfers, two billion each, Jake, Miles, and Mel. An extra thank you, Mel from Mr Dupont, fifty million dollars.” Oliver handed over a cheque to the Argentinian.

Bowing in appreciation. “Send my regards to Mr Dupont.”

“After this round, this place needs to be burnt! With him in it,” said Oliver, pointing at the former Paul Freidman.

Oliver Dupont walked out of the main entrance and looked up at the glowing evening sky, placing his leather Sylvester gloves over his manicured hands. “Well, Theo-James, we did it,” he whispered, climbing into his black Porsche Carrera. The engine roared, and a cloud of dust hit the track.

Mel ordered two of his security to douse the building and interior in diesel. Lighting a cigarette, Jake had the honour of throwing it into the doorway. Two black Audi A6s waited at the top of the main driveway. Five smartly dressed men walked away from the building as a huge explosion erupted.

Jake and Miles jumped into one car after shaking hands with Mel. Mel and his team sped off into a different direction and vanished.

Jake fist-bumped Miles. “A good job done!”

“Burn these clothes,” Miles said.

The Audi drove them to a run-down old motel outside of Rye. In room five, two immaculate black suits, white dress shirts, assorted silk ties, underwear, and shoes were ready for the two lawyers. Jake grabbed a wash bag that had been placed on the chipped dresser. "Okay, I'll wash up first." Opening the bag, Jake gasped. "Designer shower gel?"

"Compliments from the boss!" Miles laughed.

"Dupont?"

"You got it!" Laughed Miles.

"All the time I was working for Sebastian?"

"WJ, my dad William, Theo-James Miller, and Benedict Shaw are underworld!" explained Miles.

"I knew pops was a gangster when I got roped into spying on Freidman. When pops died, I had to take his place in *The Society*." Jake said. "I never knew Sebastian was part of it."

"All began in LA, 1936."

"The Godfather, Theo-James Miller?"

"Octavian-Stanley Miller, then Theo!"

Jake sat down on the corner of his fresh bed. "I knew I was working for Theo and pops, but…"

Miles joined his friend and slumped down next to Jake. "All I know is that Miller was a very powerful man. Eleanor ran away from England with him, and he threatened Viscount Templeton with his life!"

"The Templeton-Jones family didn't cut her off?"

"It was Theo all along."

"How did he become powerful?" Jake asked.

"His dad was a powerful guy in the gold trade and became owner of Miller-Lion Film Corporation. Theo-James was the golden boy, young director. Spent more time in bed with his actresses than in the chair, until he met Eleanor."

"And pops fit in because he was his friend." Jake asked, intrigued.

"My dad was a film writer, hidden behind the scenes because of his colour." Jake shook his head in disgust. Miles carried on, "Your dad was the youngest, studying law. Theo wanted a personal lawyer. My dad was his personal screenwriter to produce his movies. You're going to ask me about Benedict? He negotiated Theo's contracts, with his fists."

"The perfect team!" Jake said. "How did Dupont get involved?"

"Sebastian worked for EZM as a clerk at the age of seventeen. Worked under Freidman. He also became Earl Westwood's fascination."

"The director?"

"Yes, Earl was a close friend of Theo's. University in London called out to Dupont, and he moved there permanently. Earl sent his men over to bring Sebastian back to LA. Under Theo-James's protection Sebastian remained in London. Earl Westwood suddenly died, and his entire estate went to Dupont."

"Weren't his parents rich?"

"Yes, film director, David Jackman-Grace and actress, Martha Thomas Kernell. Very close to the Templeton-Millers. Sebastian returned to LA and took his job with EZM who became Green Records.... You know the rest."

"Wow.!"

"He met Oliver Montrose in 1959. Oliver's father owned *Conception Magazine.* Sebastian's real name is Peter Kernell."

Jake looked at Miles. "And Theo?"

"Yes, Sebastian worked under Theo and became Theo's second-in-command. Dupont is a very powerful man!"

Jake stood up with his wash bag. "How do you know all of this?"

Miles laughed. "My dad kept a journal in the family safe. I read it, locked it in my bank vault. Dad always said it would make a great film."

****

Castrum Place - Rye - New York

2nd November 2006 - 9.00 a.m.

Fire crews continued to spray water onto the fast-moving flames that were ripping down the remains of Castrum Place. The fire chief climbed over the smoking rubble, wearing protective equipment and a breathing apparatus.

One crew member raised his hand. Detective Joe Monroe shouted, “What’s the problem?”

A fire official sprinted over to the cordoned area. “Two bodies!”

Joe Monroe whistled for the forensic team to come closer. “When can we move in?”

“No way. We’ll get our guys to remove the bodies. It’s still too dangerous.”

“Do you know the cause?” Monroe asked, placing both hands on his hips.

“Looks like a gas explosion, but there is a smell of fuel?”

“Arson!”

“Or someone really can’t cook.”

Monroe turned towards a blonde middle-aged woman.

“Boss, can we go in?” she said, pulling on her forensic suit.

Monroe shook his head. “Too dangerous. This is Paul Freidman’s place.” Monroe said, looking at the smoking rubble.

“Was!” she replied.

“Two bodies?”

“Probably hookers,” she said, observing the scene with Monroe.

“Thugs?” he surmised.

“Freidman was linked to the Moulin death. Wife went missing in the Caribbean. Templeton’s record company sacked him!”

“Hookers?” Monroe smirked.

“I heard he was a sex addict.”

“Is that what you call it! I thought it was just sex when you felt like it.”

“Businessman always left this place the next morning.”

“Don’t tell me they were having brunch!” laughed Monroe.

“Well, I wouldn’t touch the sausage!” she said, walking off towards her truck.

****

City Mortuary - Rye - New York

2nd November 2006 - 3.00 p.m.

Detective Joe Monroe stood behind a glass window. A two-way speaker allowed the pathologist and the detective to speak. Two bodies lay separately covered with a white sheet on metal slabs.

The mortuary technicians prepared the first body for identification, pulling away the sheet. Joe Monroe scrunched his face at the scene that lay before him. A voice echoed over the speaker. "Detective, the dental records match a Mr Paul Freidman, body one. With so little tissue remaining, it's impossible to investigate the cause of death."

Monroe pressed the button and spoke into the intercom. "What about the other one?"

The voice crackled again. "Same COD, no dental match."

"Poor bastard," Monroe mumbled leaving the mortuary viewing room.

Walking into the bright sunlight, Monroe placed his sunshades over his squinting eyes. Lighting up a cigarette, Monroe inhaled. Facing the grey apex, ridge roof building he sighed. "Back to square one!" he muttered, climbing into his unmarked patrol car.

****

Rye - New York - 2nd November 2006 - 7.00 p.m.

Four miles from Rye State Park, a dilapidated wooden motel sat abandoned along the crumbling highway. The 690

Motel displayed one Ford Explorer parked in its gravelled parking lot, while the reception light beamed bright against the night sky.

Dust and flying gravel exploded into the atmosphere from a fierce roaring sound that shook the parking lot. A black Porsche Carrera pulled next to the Ford. The driver's window of the Porsche fell, and a hand passed over a chunky brown envelope. "All the reports done?" Oliver Dupont said.

"All done, boss," the voice responded.

"Good!" Oliver grinned and pulled up his driver's window. Reversing the Porsche at high speed, Oliver stopped the car by the motel's mailbox and slid another brown package into the green metal box. Hitting the accelerator, the Porsche scrambled for the highway and disappeared into the night.

Fire chief Doug Sume opened the envelope and began to count one-hundred-dollar bills.

****

Rye Police Headquarters - New York

3rd November 2006 - 10.00 a.m.

Hustle and bustle, telephones ringing, and people shouting were typical of Detective Joe Monroe's office. Glaring into his desktop computer, Monroe groaned.

"What's the problem?" Detective Lee said from the opposite side of the scattered paperwork.

"I don't get it! The fire report, accidental gas leak." Monroe said, confused.

"So, Freidman's death is accidental?"

"Looks that way…"

"What about the two bodies?"

"Butler and Freidman," Monroe shrugged.

Lee walked around the table and sat on the corner of the desk. "Look, it's obvious Freidman was the cutthroat killer. We call it a suicide. Case closed."

Monroe looked up at the dark-haired cop. "Case closed?"

"Drinks are on me."

Monroe sighed. "I've been reading about Freidman. Top guy in the recording world. Allison Templeton-Miller's manager."

"Mancini," Lee corrected.

"Whatever."

CHAPTER 16

Montana House - Chelsea - London

4th November 2006 - 10.00 a.m.

Pacing against the green paisley carpet, Belinda Ross-Belling Davis begged Charles for her forgiveness. Charles remained calm, sitting in his leather fireside armchair, not answering the panic-stricken redhead.

A week previously Belinda had miscarried their child and Charles was left devasted. Belinda showed no emotion whatsoever, which infuriated Charles. Still grieving, he had decided that he did not love Belinda and he had been trapped.

"I am sorry Belinda, but I do not love you."

Belinda raged. "Why, because I lost the baby?"

"I never loved you."

"So, all of this was for the baby?" She continued to pace.

Charles stared at the heavy brown velvet curtains tied back, revealing the white sash windows.

Belinda glared at him. "You love her. Everyone loves her!"

"To whom are you referring?" Charles asked in his English accent.

"Alice…Templeton!" Belinda snarled.

"Alice is happily married."

"I was happily married, until you came along!"

Charles scratched his untrimmed beard. "A woman like you could never be happy."

"Donny loved me. Me!" She pointed at herself.

"Is that why he's suing you?"

"I thought we could get married, now I'm divorced, and we can try for another baby," Belinda said.

"Marriage? Don't flatter yourself."

"Was the sex not good enough?"

"You have seven days to pack your bags. Starting yesterday."

****

Belling House - Los Angeles

4th November 2006 - 2.00 a.m.

George Krust lifted the receiver of the bedside telephone. "Yeah!" he grunted.

Rolling onto her back beside him was Melinda Ross-Belling-Krust. Sleeping, camouflaged beneath a white eye mask, Melinda shuddered when George gently rocked her.

"Honey, phone call," he said, drowsy.

"Who is it?" she mumbled.

"Belinda," he announced, falling back onto his grey satin pillow.

Removing the elasticated white sleep mask, she squinted as she switched on the side lamp. Seizing the receiver from her bedside telephone, Melinda mumbled. "Belinda, whatever is the matter?"

"Mom, it's terrible Charles has left me!" a familiar squealing voice resonated from the other side.

Pulling herself out of bed, Melinda shuffled against her Victorian flooring. Wearing her pink satin pyjamas, she fumbled for the light switch. Stumbling towards her desk, she knocked over a Charles Montgomery lamp. Eventually sitting at her mahogany desk, she picked up the telephone handset.

"Talk to me!" she muffled into her desk phone.

"Charles doesn't want to be with me because I lost the baby. I have a week to find a new place!" Belinda sobbed.

"That is disgusting. Come home!" Melinda became alert to her daughter's sobs.

"No, I want my life in England…I have a chance of work here." Belinda fibbed.

"I can wire you cash. How much?"

"Twenty-five thousand pounds." Belinda changed her attitude from sobs to delight.

"Okay, I will sort this. Please stay in touch. I will need your new address," Melinda said, observing her extravagant diamond wedding ring, sparkling from the overhead pendant lighting.

"Okay, mom. Thanks." Belinda rung off.

Melinda didn't get the chance to say goodbye.

****

Raven Realtor - Park Lane - London

4th November 2006 - 1.00 p.m.

Seated in a gold-gilt upholstered chair, a grey-haired gentleman offered his client two brochures. Crossing his legs, he spoke richly. "Madam, The Pembrokeshire Apartment, I recommend has the primary viewing."

A pinstriped Belinda accepted the brochures and smiled. Observing the literature, she commented, "Does the apartment block have a pool?"

"Madam, we are not living in the USA. London takes pride of its valuable space."

Belinda scowled. "What the hell does that mean?"

"No," he replied, checking his pocket watch. "Timothy can escort you to the premises within the next hour."

"How much is the first apartment?" Belinda smiled, crossing her legs, and sitting further back into her seat.

"Seventy-eight thousand per annum. A deposit of six thousand pounds."

"Can I take a short-term contract?"

The agent glared over the top of his spectacles. "Yes, three months is the required minimum."

“I only require the apartment for eight weeks, but I can pay the three months.”

“Yes, madam. Have you got plans after that?” he enquired.

“Eight weeks and I will have achieved my goal. Twenty-four thousand pounds. I will take the apartment,” smiled Belinda.

“You haven’t viewed it, Madam.”

“I don’t need to. When can I have the keys?”

“Tomorrow, if the funds are cleared.”

“They’re cleared,” she said, holding her hand out “Where do I sign?”

****

The Pembrokeshire Apartment - Knightsbridge London

10th November 2006 - 9.00 a.m.

Belinda strutted around her apartment barefoot, searching through luggage that lay abandoned on the wooden flooring. With its beautiful, vaulted ceilings and natural brick walls, Belinda had already wrecked the place.

Slouching against her antique furnishings, she scrambled towards a green suede clutch bag thrown against the freestanding tub. Opening the zipper, she squealed, “I’ve got you!”

Running into the sitting room, she dashed towards a stylish mid-century desk and grabbed her mobile. Placing herself on top of the desk, she swung her legs against the wood grain. Wearing just a satin cream bra and thong, she spoke into her mobile. "Hi, can I speak to Hugo Towersand, please?"

An elegant voice answered. "May I ask who is requesting his presence?"

Belinda pulled her phone away from her ear and scowled at her mobile. "What?" she mouthed. "Belinda Ross-Belling-Davis. Tell him it's the redhead he was chasing at Dickie's wedding."

A loud sigh could be heard through the speaker. "Yes Miss Davis."

Suddenly an aristocratic voice loudly reverberated against Belinda's earpiece. "Ha, the redhead. How are you faring my little minx?"

"Hugo, wonderful to hear you." Belinda pulled her face.

"Yes, I wondered how long Garrett would keep you away from me! So, he has left me the leftovers. The bastard!" He laughed.

Belinda laughed too, clueless. "I thought we..."

"Sure, be over in two hours!" he chuckled.

"Over where?"

"Towersand House. Sussex, of course!" laughed Hugo.

"How far?"

"I will send you, my driver. What is your address?"

Belinda jumped off her desk, ran into the kitchen, and grabbed the brochure. "The Pembrokeshire Apartments, Knightsbridge." She answered.

"My beautiful filly, Knightsbridge! You are a good breed. Bring an overnight bag; I may not be able to drive you back home tonight. And wear something sexy!"

****

Towersand House - West Sussex

10th November 2006 - 1.30 p.m.

Dressed in a satin black slip dress, Belinda crossed her legs in the back of the polished Bentley. Revealing her lace stocking tops, she smiled seductively at the chauffeur observing her through his rear-view mirror.

Wearing a fake fur black coat, she pulled from her pocket a compact mirror and applied sheer red lipstick onto her moist, swollen lips.

Belinda looked outside from the rear passenger window and was bowled over by the size of the building. Towersand House had over two hundred rooms. Situated in ornamental gardens it displayed nobility of a high standing.

The car pulled outside the entrance doors as a butler and maid elegantly walked down the crafted steps. The driver opened the passenger door, and Belinda stepped out. Wearing her knee-length faux fur and her red hair in an up-do, she looked glamourous.

Standing in the huge foyer, another butler anticipated her presence. Belinda handed him her coat and followed another household staff into the sitting room. Standing next to the fire was Hugo. Dressed in jeans and an open neck shirt, the short grey-haired man beamed in delight.

"Belinda, my little minx!"

"Hugo!" she smiled.

Hugo undressed her with his eyes. Noticing Belinda's sizeable breasts through her short dress, he offered her a glass of chilled white wine. Sitting opposite one another by the fire, Belinda crossed her long legs, revealing her laced stocking tops. Hugo was becoming over heated and proposed lunch.

Inside the luxurious dining room, two places were set at the bottom of a sixty-seater table. A bouquet of fresh wildflowers segregated the two diners. Staff dressed in their day suits stood back when the soup was served.

"Do your staff always watch you eat?" she said, scooping her spoon into the delicious leek soup.

"They're just being polite," he smiled.

Belinda observed his features more closely. Hugo was quite handsome for a man of sixty-four.

"I would like them to leave," Belinda said.

"Why, my little minx?" he replied, swallowing his soup.

"I must talk with you in private," she said.

Hugo placed his spoon down and ushered away his staff. "I will ring for our next course."

Belinda leaned into the table a little more, revealing her sizable cleavage bulging from her low-cut dress. Hugo could only focus on Belinda's baps instead of his own soup rolls.

"Hugo, what do you want from me?" she seductively said, licking her soup spoon.

"You," Hugo gulped. "I want you!"

Belinda licked her lips slowly with her tongue.

"I am looking for a wife. I require a beauty to walk along on my arm, someone good in bed who will drop everything when I ask!" He grinned, eating his soup again.

"Do you think that I fit that profile?"

"Yes."

"That is why you felt my arse at the wedding?"

"Yes."

"Why you left me your number."

"Yes. I knew you wouldn't last with Garrett. He's weak. That singer husband of yours is weak. You need breeding!"

"Breeding!" Belinda grinned. "You will have to show me."

Hugo shot up, patted his mouth with his napkin, and walked around the table. Pulling Belinda up from her chair, he gently kissed her neck. Pushing into him, she moaned. Hugo slid his hand up her slinky dress.

Hugo smiled. "Are we ready for our second course?"

****

On the 17th of December 2006, Belinda Ross-Belling-Davis became Lady Belle Towersand. Hugo and Belinda were married at a private chapel in Towersand village. The only people that attended were the household staff as witnesses.

Hugo had instructed Belinda not to wear any panties underneath her ivory fishtail wedding dress. When they returned to Towersand House, Hugo pounced on his new wife, consummating their marriage.

Belinda loved it; sex was so exciting with Hugo. The couple never expressed their love for one another but enjoyed erotic sex together. Hugo constantly reminded his wife of her place and it tamed Belinda's attitude to normality.

CHAPTER 17

Mancini Mansion - New Jersey

27th March 2007 - 1.00 a.m.

Davis strolled out of guest room number ten, wearing his green disposable apron. Romano paced in, distressed. "How is she?"

"She's not fully dilated yet. Go and have a coffee. We'll let you know…"

"Romano, come here," Allison blurted. "Thanks, Davis. You would think that this baby was his!"

Romano walked up to Allison.

"Down the steps!" She pointed at him. "Hush. We have Autumn asleep in the nursery, and you are speaking far too loudly in the passageway."

Autumn now five months old, slept in her yellow teddy bear nursery with an adjoining door to her parents' room.

Allison and Romano had supervised builders and designers to refashion ten guestrooms into elegant nurseries, and master bedrooms.

Allison refused to disturb her staff, so she marched into the kitchen and made Earl Grey. "Sit!" she ordered Romano and pointed towards the huge preparation island.

"Alice?"

"The twins will be delivered soon. My God! What is wrong with you?" she snarled.

"Baby, I'm sorry for upsetting you. I just..."

"Can't wait?"

"Sarah-Jane will be okay." Allison sat down opposite her husband.

"Belinda?" Romano softly spoke.

"Sarah-Jane disowned her mother months ago," Allison said, sipping her hot tea.

"Can I say one thing?" Romano walked his fingers towards Allison's hand.

"Go on…"

"I love you when you are bossy!"

Allison tutted. "I must say, Autumn loves you. How's the book going?"

"Well, I'll have to mention Belinda!"

"Go ahead. Not like she can read!" Allison sniggered.

****

Sebastian Jr paced into the kitchen and dropped onto a vacant leather stool "I can't cope with this!"

Allison reached out and held his hand. "It is very stressful, but you should be with her!"

"Seb, mom's right, you need to be with your wife." Romano grabbed an empty mug and walked over to the percolator. Pouring steaming black coffee into the mug, Romano slid the drink over towards his son.

"How is she?" Allison asked the question, stroking Sebastian's hand.

"She's okay, it's me!"

Laughing, Allison looked at the double act sat in front of her. "Definitely like father, like son!"

****

Sarah-Jane shuffled around the bedroom, clutching her back.

"Sarah, do you want any Diamorphine?" Maxi asked, timing Sarah's movement with his pocket watch.

"No."

The bedroom door opened. "Alice!" Davis and Maxi said.

Pacing over to Sarah-Jane, Allison observed her struggling daughter-in-law. "Run the bath!" She gestured towards the two doctors.

Maxi looked puzzled at the request.

"Do it!" Allison scowled.

Davis rushed into the bathroom and turned on the hot water faucet, while Allison helped Sarah-Jane with her breathing.

“Sarah-Jane, do you have anything under your nightgown?” she asked.

Sarah nodded.

“Right. We are going to put you in the bath. It will relax you, okay?”

Davis and Maxi assisted Allison with transferring Sarah from the bedroom into the tub. Checking the water first, Allison said, “Lift her right in.”

The warmth of the water soothed Sarah-Jane’s body. With a slight groan, she laid back in the tub.

“Alice?” Maxi said.

“Water birth. My grandchildren are going to be born in water. Autumn-Marie was my first water baby,” Allison reminisced. “Disposable apron and gloves!”

“Gloves?” Maxi was interrupted.

“My mansion, my rules!” She cut in. Wearing her black leggings and long-sleeved t-shirt, Allison removed her flipflops and knelt at the side of the bath, assuring Sarah-Jane she was doing okay.

Within an hour, a trace of blood circled above the delicate ripples of water. Davis made his way over to her side. “Sarah, push!”

Sarah pushed while Allison held her hand. Davis grabbed a baby girl. Pulling her from the water, Maxi examined her.

Davis cut the umbilical cord and called out to Sarah "Push harder!"

Heaving with everything she had, Maxi pulled out another baby girl. Allison wept with joy, cuddling baby number one hidden within a fluffy towel, while Maxi examined baby number two.

After Sarah-Jane's placenta was removed, she needed to be showered. Allison was on it. Cries bellowed around the bathroom as Allison helped Sarah-Jane into the walk-in shower. The twins cried in Davis and Maxi's arms in the next room.

Rushing out of the bathroom, Allison searched through the farmhouse-style country drawers for Sarah-Jane's night clothes. "Who organized these drawers!"

Maxi and Davis swaddled the screaming babies in fresh clothes. "Where is Sebastian? "They both said.

Footfalls burst into the peach-coloured bedroom. Romano, Sebastian, and Donny looked around the carnage in awe. Allison turned around and pointed at Romano. "You, go into the kitchen and get two bottles of formula!"

Romano froze. "Which cupboard?"

"The baby cupboard, dummy!" She grabbed Sebastian and Donny by their arms. "Diapers and baby grow in that bottom drawer. Now!" she howled.

Not having time to observe the new-borns, the three males scattered in different directions, while Allison attended to Sarah-Jane in the bathroom.

"Glad you're here, Alice!" Sarah said, pouring lavender shower cream onto her pale body.

"I noticed the new-born diapers and baby grows while I was looking for your nightwear."

"Seb was supposed to do all of that."

"Men are only good at fertilizing," Allison scoffed.

"Rup was really good with Rachel."

"Sebastian and Nathaniel are just like their father. Don't worry, he will be a good dad!" smiled Allison, holding out a huge bath sheet.

Allison dressed Sarah-Jane into her cotton flowered underwear and pyjamas. Sitting at the vanity, Allison brushed Sarah's long red hair. "I remember when I used to brush your mom's hair when we were kids. You have the same colour."

Sarah stared at Allison in the double illuminating mirrors. "Do you miss her?"

Allison looked at Sarah and put both hands on her shoulders. "No. Never miss anyone who wouldn't miss you."

Sarah-Jane grabbed Allison's hand, still facing the mirror. "I don't miss her."

Allison bent down and placed a delicate kiss on Sarah's cheek. Allison turned towards the door and watched both babies being dressed into their lemon baby grows.

Sebastian and Donny sat on the king-sized floral bed, feeding baby one and baby two. Romano supervised, positioning Sebastian's hand on the bottle.

Allison beamed. "Sarah, do you have any names yet?"

"Eleanor Grace Templeton-Mancini and Allison Jane Templeton-Mancini."

"Perfect!"

****

Aquifolium Mansion - New Jersey

21st November 2010

Demonstrating its magnificence and power, the fabulous home of Sebastian and Oliver Dupont towered into the evening sky. Assorted sports cars parked outside where cool lighting escaped through arched windows onto the black adobe brickwork drive.

Oliver Dupont sat in his comfortable throne chair positioned at the end of a round table. Medieval candle arbours sat in the centre of the twenty-seater table.

Jake Pullman, Miles Peterson, Craig Welling, and Oliver chatted between one another. The double doors opened, and their mouths shut. Rupert Templeton-Mancini walked into the dining room with Jono Murrey and took his place next to

Craig Welling. Following Rupert, three more males entered with their bodyguards.

"I have called this meeting today because alternate objectives have created a movement in positions," Oliver announced. "The plan of action will consist of the following..."

Jake stood up and strolled around the table, handing each gentleman a file.

"Please open to page two." Oliver calmly said.

Rupert opened his file and grinned. Glancing over at him was thirty-year-old Daniel Templeton-Miller. Daniel, now a criminal lawyer, worked for Jake Pullman and was named as a partner in 2009. Unmarried but extremely rich, he used it to his advantage.

Thirty-year-old Andrew La-Mount-Martinez flipped through his file. Working in the financial sector gained him great opportunities. Married to Penelope Tomkinson-Clifton, the couple struggled to conceive their first child. IVF was their next course of action.

Jack Welling winked at his father from the across the round table. The twenty-four-year-old was handsome, tall, and muscular. Jack, also a criminal lawyer, worked for Jake.

"I will be operating this side of the business now that Mr Dupont is retiring. Miles is my legal, and Craig is the negotiator. If anyone has a problem with that, please remember that my security is armed."

"If our team disperse for any reason, Rupert will become the controller or the influencer."

Jack broke in. "Godfather!"

Oliver sighed. "We do not like to use that term! The three top guys, legal, financial and negotiator: Daniel, Andrew, and you, Jack."

All three nodded. Oliver Dupont continued on with the conversation. "In 2011, the Mancini triplets will be taking over ownership of Miller-Sphere Films."

"Alice?" Jack interrupted.

"Retiring from Miller-Sphere." Oliver said pointing at Rupert. "You, my boy, will control the enterprise over your brothers! Pillion Filming Productions are already trying to sabotage Miller-Sphere."

Daniel cut in. "How?"

"Negative reviews, delaying actors..."

"Delaying actors?" Daniel repeated.

"*Nobody Better* was delayed by four weeks, cost Miller-Sphere thousands. Pillion was paying Willie Yang two million in cash to delay his movie."

"So, what is the plan?" Rupert said.

"We bankrupt Pillion, buy them out, and we invest Pillion into Miller-Sphere." Oliver smiled.

The suited men glanced towards Andrew La-Mount-Martinez. “I can crash Pillion’s shares!”

“Good man!” Sebastian took his seat in the available throne chair positioned opposite Oliver.

Sebastian held onto his cane while he rested against his high cushioned chair. “Cripple Pillion. As for CEO Danny Decco, shoot him if you must!”

“Your orders, Sebastian?” Rupert said.

“No, mine!” A female voice erupted from the entrance. Allison took an empty chair next to Sebastian. “I will be running this operation. “I am your new controller. You have all been sworn into *The Society*…I take it, you are all ready for your first job?” Allison tapped her long painted fingernails against the table. “Good. My father ran *The Society* in 1936 under the guidance of my grandfather. It shall remain within the Templeton-Miller empire.”

****

Mancini Mansion - New Jersey

31st December 2010 - 1.00 p.m.

Seated in her contemporary conservatory drinking Earl Grey, Allison smiled at four-year-old Autumn Marie running and dancing in her pink ballerina costume. With her long black curling hair and olive skin, she portrayed an original Mancini.

Rachel laughed at her daughter's poor pirouette. "She will be a dancer when she grows up."

Allison disagreed. "An actress, like her grandmama!"

"I believe these two will be actresses," laughed Sarah-Jane, pointing at her identical twin daughters Eleanor and Allison.

Allison smiled while the twins blew large rainbow-shaped bubbles. Both girls had long, black hair and olive skin. Sarah-Jane thought one child would be a redhead, like herself, but the Mancini genes were too strong.

Joining the twins and their bubble machine were three-year-old Romano Christian (Nathaniel's son) and three-year-old Theo-James (Ella-Louisa's son). The two boys were of Mancini colouring and attitude.

Heavily pregnant with baby number four, Ella burped into her tissue. "Sorry, I have got so much wind with this baby."

Allison laughed. "Another boy?"

"No!" Ella selected a piece of lemon cake.

Dickie strolled into the conservatory with his sons William-Sebastian, aged two and a half, and Nathaniel-Paul, aged eighteen months. "What are you giggling at?"

Ella burped again.

"It's a boy!" Rachel giggled.

Sitting on a vacant wicker sofa, Dickie released both of his sons while they ran towards their brother, squealing. "She is going to have another if this baby is not a girl!"

Sarah-Jane stopped chewing her cake. "Really! Five babies?"

Ella continued to gulp down her lemon cake. "We need a girl to break up the masculinity in the house!"

Dickie laughed. "More kids the better!"

"We are sticking at one," Rachel cut in. "Rupert's very busy with his filming and now he's going to be president of Miller-Sphere Films!"

"Two for us," Sarah-Jane sighed. "Seb is useless."

Allison leaned back against her chair and observed her family growing. Romano was on a book tour with his biography called *How I Caught a Falling Star*. She wasn't too impressed with the title because it made her feel has though, she had been failing. In Romano's thinking, it was a falling star from the sky into his heart.

****

Mancini Mansion - New Jersey

31st December 2010 - 10.00 p.m.

The family enjoyed brandy and assorted drinks while chatting and laughing together. The children were sound asleep in their nurseries. Ella-Louisa had retired early with her husband Dickie.

Ringing sounded from the brass telephone in the hallway. Simpson walked into the vast burgundy sitting room. “Miss Alice, the police would like a word.”

Allison remained calm. Standing up from the Chesterfield suite, she walked into the foyer.

Jono Murrey walked into the foyer with two uniformed police officers. Flashing lights from their squad car lit up Mancini Mansion, while snow fell onto the surrounding driveway.

“Romano!” Allison said.

Jono held Allison’s hand. “There’s been an accident.”

“He’s dead. I know, I can feel it!” Allison covered her heart with her hand. “He didn’t make it for dinner.”

Sebastian and Oliver appeared behind Allison. “What happened?”

“Jet hit a snowstorm over the Atlantic,” replied a uniformed officer.

Sebastian grabbed Allison. “My office, all of you!”

The family remained silent, trying to observe the hushed conversation in the foyer. Sebastian escorted Allison, Jono, and the uniformed officers into his office.

Placing herself onto a Chesterfield sofa, Allison began to sob. “He’s in the water!”

Sebastian ran across to Allison with a glass of brandy. “Alice, drink this.”

Allison downed the entire contents. “He’s not coming home.”

“He’s dead, Alice.” Jono said.

“Don’t use the d-word!” Sebastian warned.

“How much will it cost to find him and the crew? Remember, they were our staff, and they have families of their own!” She continued to sob.

“Alice!” Sebastian gripped her hand.

“I’ve already lost Maria and Giuseppe. Now I have lost my husband, their son!”

“Alice!” Sebastian desperately tried to calm her.

“I want another drink.” She held out her empty glass towards Sebastian.

“I will sort this!” Sebastian said.

After an hour Jono and the uniformed officers left the office. Allison drank another brandy and removed herself from Sebastian’s sofa, wiping her eyes.

Following her dainty steps into the foyer, Sebastian said, “You are in shock, Alice. Let Oliver and I tell the children.”

Turning around, she glared at her friend. “Don’t you dare!”

The atmosphere fell into silence and Allison paced into the sitting room. Her hardness cut into the confusion of her friends and family. Looking at her four children and their spouses, she calmly said, "There has been an accident. Your father is no longer with us."

Shock hit their faces like this was the big joke of the night. Sarah-Jane burst into tears while Sebastian Jr grabbed his wife and held her in his arms. Rachel and Rupert remained silent. Nathaniel began to weep.

Adele, Helen, and Lucinda ran up to Allison and hugged her. "Are you okay?" they whispered into her hair.

"Today when I spoke to him, I knew it was going to be my last conversation with him." She stared blankly into the roaring fire; tears gently trickled down her face.

Maxi, Jake, Craig, and Donny hugged the Mancini siblings. Withholding their grief, the guys maintained their strength towards the brothers.

"Ella-Louisa!" Oliver stepped in.

Allison turned away from her girlfriends. "Dickie will have to tell her. She can't afford to lose the baby."

****

Mancini Mansion - New Jersey

1st January 2011 - 3.00 a.m.

Resting against her pillows, she cuddled Romano's dress shirt. Still fully dressed in her evening gown, she curled into a ball. "I promise, Romano," she whispered into the satin bedspread. "I will find you."

A knock at the door interrupted her sobs. “Yes?” she yelled, wiping her eyes.

Dressed in her satin green maternity nightshirt and robe, Ella-Louisa shuffled inside, carrying a tray of Earl Grey in a teapot and two china cups. “I thought this may help, mom!

“Ella, darling, you are heavily pregnant.” Allison removed herself from the four-poster bed and grabbed the tray from Ella-Louisa, “Come here, let’s have a girly chat.”

Ella made herself comfortable against Romano’s pillows whilst Allison poured the tea. Alice handed over a cup and saucer to Ella, while steam rose into the soft lighting. “You couldn’t sleep?” Allison looked at Ella, blowing her tea.

“Dickie told me…”

“You seem fine,” Allison replied.

“I believe it was dad’s time. He always spoke of death after grandmama and grandpapa died.”

“Maria and Giuseppe were beautiful people. I loved them both.” Allison sighed, wiping her eyes with a tissue.

“Dying a few months apart.” Ella looked down at her cup. “True love.”

Allison smiled, still blotchy from her sobs. “Mama and papa died within one day of one another!”

“Did grandpapa kill himself?”

“No, died of a broken heart. Like Maria.”

Ella looked at Allison in horror. "You won't die of a broken heart?"

"No! Your father was the love of my life, but I have unfinished business."

"You have become very strong over these past few years. I admire that."

Allison laughed. "I used to be a nervous wreck when I was young. My old manager told me to toughen up. Who knew it would feel like this?"

"I will miss dad! I loved him so much." Ella looked at her mother. "Who purchases a one-year-old a pink Mercedes?"

Allison nodded. "He did it with all of you! I had more smashed vases with those toy cars! Nathaniel ran over a maid's foot!"

"Nat makes me laugh, even today. Did you know he'd returned his new Bentley convertible back to the showroom?"

"Why?"

"The soft top wouldn't go down when he drove it!"

"For safety reasons. You must stop the car and then press the button to release the soft top."

"Exactly!" laughed Ella.

"Tell me about Sandura Pierce?"

Ella scoffed, still gripping her Earl Grey. "She made a pass at Nat on his new film set. He stormed off and refused to leave his trailer. Rup was not on set at the time, but he caught up with her."

"What happened?" Allison listened with interest.

"Rup sacked her. She threatened him, so Rup was going to get her charged with sexual assault."

Allison laughed. "So, it has not changed at all. Nat is a good-looking guy. Women are drawn to him. It doesn't matter if he is married or not. In the filming world it's sex that rules."

"Like you and Stephen?"

"He's a very close friend, but he does still love me and always will."

"Why did dad take years to write your biography?"

"I disagreed with a lot of his writing. Your father would refuse to write anything on the matter after we had argued."

"It's a best seller," sighed Ella.

"I'll never read it." Allison continued to drink her tea.

****

St Paul's Chapel - Zurich - Switzerland

25th March 2011 - 1.00 p.m.

Walking down the cool stone steps, Allison held onto her white rose. Wearing her black Sylvester-Montgomery suit and head veil, she observed her parents' caskets. Following her, Ella-Louisa, Sebastian, Rupert, Benedict, and Nathaniel remained silent. Allison placed a single white rose upon Romano's quartz metal casket.

Accepting his death became real for Allison in January when she located investigators to search for the Mancini jet. The weather hampered the search, and it wasn't until late January that the salvage teams could commence. On the 20th of March, they found the wreckage. Romano was still seated beside bodyguard Micky Connelly.

Providing financial support for the families, Allison appointed Bentley and Hardy to assist with Jake Pullman's team. Romano was flown to Switzerland and was laid to rest in the Templeton-Miller tomb.

Investigators blamed pilot error caused by the snowstorm, spatial disorientation. Allison tore up the report and said her final goodbye to Romano.

Walking around Templeton House rekindled childhood memories: Henry chasing her around the orchard, Richard teasing her dolls, Annie sneaking into the kitchens. The Templeton-Miller siblings still owned the house four ways and preserved its historical décor.

Amile Templeton-Miller, unmarried, lived alone in the great house. The thirty-three-year-old was an established author, writing romantic fiction from Theo-James's old office. The oil painting of Eleanor still hung on the office wall, watching.

****

Templeton House - Zurich - Switzerland

25th March 2011 - 5.00 p.m.

Bentley and Hardy held a press conference outside the gates of Templeton House. Sebastian Dupont walked around the gardens with Allison, observing the colourful blooms of spring flowers and cascading greenery.

Sebastian conversed with her, crunching on the gravelled pathway. "How are you faring, my darling?"

"I can relax now that he's at peace." She smiled under her huge black hat.

"What's next?" Sebastian asked, looking straight ahead.

"Tuscany. I now own the Mancini vineyards. I will pass them onto Sebastian and Sarah-Jane when I die." Allison shuddered. "I would like you and Oliver to accompany me on my trip. I am also taking Stephen Golding."

Sebastian cleared his throat. "Why?"

"After Fran, he had nothing in life but work. I'm glad Romano and Stephen became friends in the end."

"You are?"

"Stop! No, there was only Romano." She sighed.

Sebastian glared. “Alice, I hope you don’t meet him too soon…”

“Sebastian, I have the vineyards to organise. Also, I have my new grandson, Charles. Ella’s trying for a little girl!”

“My God. Five?”

“Well, more than four. Benedict and Leon are together now, and the world has accepted them. They want children too!”

Sebastian dropped his cane. “How?”

“Surrogacy. Benedict and Leon’s biology.”

“Sounds complicated,” huffed Sebastian.

Sebastian sat down on a vintage bench by the side of the gravel pathway. The breeze blew his whitening hair. Tapping his cane, he sighed. “I would have loved children with Oliver, but it was a crime that two men loved one another in my day.”

Allison took her place next to him and grabbed his hand. “Hey, you can have mine!”

Sebastian smiled. “I’m glad you insisted no one cried today. Romano would have liked that.”

Allison looked at Templeton House standing in all its glory. “Shedding tears doesn’t mend a broken heart, but it does make you see things clearer.”

"You, Allison Templeton-Miller, have grown up so much since I first met you in London all those years ago. We have had a brilliant adventure, my girl!"

"Mancini, Sebastian, Templeton-Mancini."

"Hyphens, you'd think you were getting paid by the word."

Sebastian and Allison laughed, holding on to one another. Seven screaming children came running towards the pair, waving balloons. Standing up from the garden bench, she held her arms out to greet them. "There are your children, Sebastian, enjoy them because they will soon grow and leave the nest."

Bellows of laughter entered the air while Allison chased and tickled her grandchildren with the help of her long dear friend Sebastian Dupont.

CHAPTER 18

Mumbai - India - 17th October 2019

The Gateway of India exhibited its iconic structure against the blazing heat. Sixty-three-year-old Allison Templeton–Mancini and sixty-nine-year-old Stephen-Paul Golding held hands underneath the famous arch.

"I told you to wear flat shoes," he groaned.

"I'm glad you are holding my hand, or I would have fallen onto my ass!" she chuckled.

"Let's buy you some flip-flops so you can take those damn wedges off!"

"There is a market a few streets away."

"Then it's a drink! Where is Tomas?"

"He's never far away."

Allison and Stephen ran towards a *tuk-tuk*. Tomas followed the pair and waved his approval. Stepping into the vehicle, Allison laughed. "This is fun, no one knows us!"

"Well, Alice, your hair is blonde, not forgetting your grey bits!" scoffed Stephen.

"Says the guy with white hair!"

Tomas jumped into a green *tuk-tuk* behind Allison's red one. "Follow that movie star!" he ordered the driver. Squashing the six-foot-three bodyguard, dressed in shorts into the small vehicle became a challenge. The poor driver pushed the American onto the back seat with all his might.

Eventually the *tuk-tuks* set off speeding in between traffic, vibrating and shaking. Allison cried with laughter, while Stephen hung on for dear life. "This is fun!" she screamed.

"I think I'm tuk-sick!" groaned Stephen.

Horns beeped and cars swerved. The vehicle stopped. "Is this it?" Stephen grunted.

"Let's go and buy shoes!" Allison jumped out.

"I'm dying for a beer!" groaned Stephen, tipping the driver.

"You guys, okay?" A voice said behind them.

"Tomas, did you manage to fit in?" Allison smiled, looking up at her giant bodyguard.

"Only just, Miss Alice," he replied, rubbing his back.

Bustling with activity, sellers enticed Allison, Stephen, and Tomas to buy their products. Allison nodded and continued to struggle through the crowds. A small and gentle man carrying shoes tied to a lengthy piece of rope collided with the superstar. Nearly knocking him over, Allison held one finger up and pointed to a pair of brown leather flip-flops. Scrambling for his stock, he smiled and untied the pair that Allison had selected.

Placing the flip-flops onto her feet, she offered him double his asking price. The man bowed in appreciation.

Interrupting the exciting moment, Stephen cut in. “Drink!”

Tomas shouted above the crowds, “Follow me!”

The couple followed the bodyguard through the crowds. Suddenly finding themselves on a street exhibiting luxury buildings and greenery, Tomas continued to pace towards a white building displaying a spraying fountain.

“We’re here!” Tomas grinned.

Observing the beautiful surroundings, Allison replied, “Where is here?”

“Hotel Saanvi.”

“I know this place. It is where I first…” Stephen trailed off.

Allison grabbed his arm. “Fran stayed here a long time ago.”

“Back then it was called Kabir,” he muttered, observing the elegant scene. “Not changed a great deal, but…”

“But it still shows its style and grace!” Allison finished his sentence. “Come on, let’s get a drink.” Grabbing Stephen’s hand, she tugged him towards the grand entrance.

Decked in elegance and opulence the exquisite wooden furniture and architecture amazed Allison. Silver polished tile flooring, tiered water fountains and greenery completed the design.

Tomas spoke with a beautiful receptionist standing at the glossy bamboo desk. Waving at Allison and Stephen, Tomas followed the well-attired female out into the gardens.

Stepping into majestic gardens with long stretches of cascading fountains, Allison breathed in the atmosphere. Placing themselves at an aluminium dining table, she and Stephen ordered their drinks from a uniformed waiter. Tomas absconded into oblivion with the attractive receptionist.

"Do you think Tomas knows the female who brought us here?" Allison enquired.

"Probably," grinned Stephen.

"Lovers," Allison said. Listening to the sound of chirping parakeets and magpie-robins, she sighed. "I feel at peace here."

"You have always adored Mumbai or Bombay, as it was."

"My favourite place in the whole wide world." She said, accepting her glass of red wine from the waiter.

"Alice, do you like our holidays together?" Stephen said between sips of whiskey.

"I do. It's a shame you cannot ski," she laughed, observing an English couple taking their place behind

Stephen. Leaning across the table, she whispered. “I hope the couple behind you doesn’t recognise us.”

“Alice, you ended your show biz career years ago.”

“Allison Templeton-Mancini will never end! Look at Dillion Enero. I sold more albums than him!” she scoffed.

“Dillion isn’t a musician, Alice. Dillion is a 1960’s God.”

Absorbing the suns heat and tranquillity, Stephen and Allison laughed, enjoying their memorable afternoon. Happy spending their time together, the two film stars recollected old times.

****

Jammu Hotel - Mumbai - India

17th October 2019 - 8.00 p.m.

The night sky reflected the distant city lights. Allison strolled onto the balcony wearing her bandeau silver evening dress. Leaning against the stone balcony wall, wearing cream dress trousers and a white cotton dress shirt, stood Stephen-Paul Golding.

“Alice, you look beautiful.” He offered her a glass of champagne.

“Thank you, Stephen. You look cool,” she laughed. “I think my outfit is wrong for these temperatures!”

“You always look a million dollars, rain or shine.” He clinked his glass against hers.

The couple walked over to a table, covered with a white linen tablecloth and crockery. A waiter dressed in a tuxedo passed Allison and Stephen a leather menu.

Accepting her menu, she smiled at the poor waiter who must have been melting in the torrid heat.

"What do you fancy?" Stephen said.

"Japanese."

"You don't look Japanese!"

"Chinese?"

"Why don't you just have a mixed menu?" Stephen mumbled into his menu.

"Peking Duck!"

"Gourmet Hamper for me. I'm having everything!" Stephen grinned, laying his menu flat on the table.

"You sound like it is your last supper," Allison laughed.

Stephen remained quiet. The waiter appeared at the silent table and took the couple's order. Allison looked suspicious at Stephen and continued to play with her champagne glass.

"Beautiful night," he said, breaking the silence.

"It is," she replied back observing her bubbles rising to the top of her glass.

"I'm starved."

"Okay, Stephen. Spill the beans!"

"If you want beans, order some," Stephen insisted.

Allison looked away. "How can I eat when I know you are holding something back?"

"Alice, I'm dying."

"We are all dying," scoffed Allison, becoming frustrated.

Stephen grabbed her left hand and looked directly into her deep brown eyes. "Cancer. I have weeks to live."

Allison went pale. "Oh no, Stephen," she whispered, gripping his hand back. "I'm so sorry."

"I have already accepted it. I just didn't know how to tell you."

"Where is your cancer?"

"Does it matter? No crying!" He suddenly pointed at her.

Her tears swelled. Grabbing her fabric napkin, she dabbed her eyes. Black mascara smudged.

"Treatment, did you have treatment?"

"It's too late. I was surprised. I thought with all the sex I had in my lifetime the risks would have been lower."

"You have prostate cancer. That's an old wives' tale," Allison sniffled.

"Everything is sorted…W & J Pullman are my executors."

"Jake!"

"It's his job."

"What isn't his job?"

“A great deal of my fortune is going to the Templeton-Mancini Foundation.”

Allison gasped. “Stephen, that is wonderful. Thank you.”

He kissed her hand. “It’s the least I could do.”

After their meal, Stephen asked Allison to dance with him on the balcony. They swayed in silence as Alice hummed *Heavenly Body* beneath the twinkling stars of Mumbai.

Later the couple had decided to walk up the stairwell instead of catching the elevator. Standing outside her elegant suite, she kissed him on his cheek. “I feel that I am saying goodbye instead of good night.”

“Alice, I’ll see you for breakfast.” He kissed her back. “Don’t worry about me. I’m not dead yet!”

Allison opened her door and strolled into her room, leaving Stephen standing outside. Shuddering, she managed to close the door behind her. Trying not to think about death, she felt a sharp pain in her head.

She ran into the bathroom and grabbed a bottled water. Opening her vanity case, she selected two aspirin and swallowed the pain killers before climbing into bed.

Allison noticed that the lights were still on. Penetrating white light filtered from the bathroom doorway. Climbing out of bed she walked towards the lit room. Suddenly a figure stepped out with long black hair and olive skin.

"Romano!" she whispered. "Oh, my Romano!"

Dressed in his tight black jeans and white dress shirt, the twenty-six-year-old smiled. "I'm back, baby."

"Romano, you are young again!" she whispered.

"You are too!"

Allison looked down at her smooth soft hands, she noticed that all the dark blemishes and wrinkles had vanished.

"Baby, I am sorry you had to endure an aneurysm, but it was the only way I could get you here."

Allison looked towards the bed and saw herself in a deep, peaceful sleep. "I'm still in bed!"

"You are," Romano smiled, holding out his masculine hand.

Allison walked towards him in the neon haze. "I said goodbye to everyone. I knew I would never go back."

Romano held her hand and pulled her up to his chest. "Stephen will be joining us next week. His time is limited." Romano placed his full, moist lips upon hers and kissed her intensely. Slightly pulling away from her, he whispered, "Are you ready?"

Allison nodded "Always."

Romano and Allison walked arm in arm into the brilliant white light while the door gently closed behind them.

Suddenly underneath the bathroom door, the light faded into darkness and the lovers vanished into eternity, forever.

The End

A supernova is a powerful and luminous stellar explosion. This astronomical event occurs during the last stages of a massive star is triggered into a nuclear fusion and destroyed. The optical luminosity of a supernova can be the size of an entire galaxy before fading over weeks or months. This event is the end of a star's life.

Farewell, Allison Templeton – Mancini.

CPSIA information can be obtained
at www.ICGtesting.com
Printed in the USA
LVHW031941030423
743357LV00015B/1457

9 781916 540392